THE SKY INSIDE

CLARE B. DUNKLE

SIMON AND SCHUSTER

ACKNOWLEDGMENTS

Special thanks to my editor, Ginee Seo,
for the passion and wisdom she
brought to our work on this book.

First published in Great Britain in 2008
by Simon & Schuster UK Ltd
Africa House, 64-78 Kingsway, London WC2B 6AH
A CBS COMPANY

Originally published in 2008 by
Atheneum Books for Young Readers
An imprint of Simon & Schuster Children's
Publishing Division, New York

Text copyright © 2008 by Clare B. Dunkle
Book design by Michael McCartney

A CIP catalogue record for this book
is available from the British Library.

ISBN: 978-1-41692-610-8

1 3 5 7 9 10 8 6 4 2

Printed by CPI Cox & Wyman, Reading, Berkshire RG1 8EX

www.simonsays.co.uk

FOR MY BIG BROTHER ANTHONY

PROLOGUE

The big television cameras of the *You've Been Caught Napping* game show prowled in the darkness at the edge of the set, their lenses focused on the old man's face. Mindlessly thorough, they relayed to viewers his iron gray hair, his thick bifocals, and the trickles of sweat that wandered down tracks of wrinkles into his eyes. A thoughtful viewer might have wondered why he didn't wipe the sweat away. But behind the silver podium that displayed a very high score, his hands lay trapped in a pair of strong plastic manacles. That was something those cameras couldn't see.

"You're right again, Dr. Church! You are simply amazing." The handsome host beamed at the old man, white teeth flashing in a tanned face. "That completes the round. What will our contestant do next? Will he take home his winnings?" The audience groaned. "Or will he try to double them with our special bonus quiz?"

The audience shouted and cheered. This was odd because no audience was there. Beyond the banks of garish lights, the cavernous studio was empty.

"It's a big decision," said the host. "He needs to think it over, and that gives us time for a commercial break. We'll be back with Dr. Rudolph Church right after this!"

The lively notes of a familiar advertising tune cut through the studio, and the wildly cheering audience hushed with the flick of a switch. The old man rested his head on the podium in front of him, the one that hid their nasty secret. After all, game shows were rollicking good fun, entertainment for the whole family. Imagine how viewers would feel if they saw the hypodermic needle inserted in his arm.

Meanwhile, in a comfortable living room, two of those viewers were fighting over the remote. The bigger one snatched it away and triumphantly changed the channel, and a buzzing squadron of red motor scooters charged across the screen.

"Martin, you jerk!" said the girl, flopping back onto the sofa. "You always watch these silly races! I wanted to see the rest of that."

"Mom says no game shows," Martin said smugly. "Plus, that one's stupid. 'Who wrote this?' 'What's the term for that?' It's as bad as school."

"I like it," Cassie said. "It teaches me things. And this contestant is amazing. He hasn't been sent off in nine straight shows."

"Big hairy deal," Martin said, leaning forward to grab her bag of chips. "Who cares what happens to one old man?"

CHAPTER ONE

The first day of spring had come to the suburb, bringing its subtle but unmistakable signs. Martin noticed them right away as he left his house that morning. The recording that played through the neighborhood speakers was different, for one thing. It had lost its spooky, desolate sound. And wiry old Mr. LaRue was kneeling on the sidewalk next door, peeling the glittering snowflakes off his big picture window and sticking a line of pink and yellow flowers there instead.

Cassie wanted to watch, so Martin loitered on the sidewalk to let her. He gazed down the curving row of redbrick houses that framed the circular street, hooked together so that the garage wall of one became the bedroom wall of the next. The houses had identical windows, identical doors, and identical garage doors. At each garage, the pale gray sidewalk slanted down to the dark gray street so that scooter wheels could roll over it. Then the curb rose again and became level until the next garage: dip, rise, dip, rise, all around the edge of the street, like a perfect piecrust.

In the center of the circle lay the park, with its wide green-gravel spaces, dusty baseball field, bonded-rubber jogging track, and brightly colored play structures. The exact middle was a fishpond where Dad went to practice casting. Once, this park had seemed like a wonderland to Martin, and it had only recently ceased to be a marvel to his six-year-old sister. Now it was just the park: a good thing, to be sure, but a place of limited joys.

"See," directed Mr. LaRue, pausing in his work to glance up at them, "see, these are roses, and these are daffodils." He unstuck an orangey yellow flower from the vinyl sheet and carefully smoothed it onto the window glass. "They're for spring. It's spring now, you know."

"The vernal equinox," Cassie agreed.

Martin was bored. He had seen a number of springs arrive, had heard the speakers change their music and watched the plastic flowers go up on front windows across the neighborhood. None of it interested him anymore. Just this year, he had begun to grow at a prodigious rate, zooming past his peers, looking down on their hair parts and cowlicks. Not one ounce of weight, it would seem, had come with this growth, so he was beginning to resemble an Elasto-doll or a spaghetti noodle. His hair was such a dark shade of brown that everyone called it black, and his eyes were such a dark hazel that they looked brown. Only when he was excited did flecks of green and gold light up in them, but that didn't happen very often. Usually, Martin was assessing life cautiously from behind lowered eyelids: thinking of ways to escape class, thinking of plausible excuses for not doing schoolwork, or thinking of the millions of things he would rather do than sit in class and do schoolwork. No spark of color lit his eyes then. "Stop looking sullen!" his teacher would snap.

Martin sighed and tilted his head back, gazing at the network of steel girders that held up the immense dome enclosing their suburb. The vast metal structure was painted pale blue with big white splotches wherever the square golden skylights didn't intrude. *Clouds*, his granny had called those white blotches. He didn't see why they needed a special name.

High above him, a tiny inconspicuous figure crawled along one of the steel beams. Blue against the enormous blue ceiling, a tool bot was checking the rivets. As it crawled onto a cloud, the robotic form stood out clearly for a few seconds. Then it paused, probably to adjust its settings, and turned white, blending in once more.

A cloudy bot was harder to see than a blue one. Martin lost it against the faint lines and seams of the dome. He felt a tug at his sleeve. Cassie wanted his attention.

"Yard work isn't for everybody," Mr. LaRue was saying, "but I take pride in it. Got my lawn all finished." He gestured at a strip of green plastic that fringed the bottom of his house's red brick. "Bennett's still got his autumn leaves up on his window. It wouldn't kill some people to do a little work around here."

"Today is Martin's birthday," Cassie said. "It's nice that the speakers are playing something pleasant."

The old man looked scornful. "Birthday's got nothing to do with it." He used a razor blade to remove the last traces of a snowflake's outline. "It's the spring song," he said, pointing his razor at the nearest hidden speaker. "That's a robin, that's what that is."

Cassie tilted her head to listen to the jaunty, careless notes. "I don't know how that can be a song," she said. "There isn't a tune. It's different every time."

"Don't contradict me!" said Mr. LaRue. "Don't you smart kids learn any manners? If I say it's a song, it's a song, and if I say it's a robin, it's a robin!"

"Let's get to school," Martin interrupted, catching Cassie by the strap on the top of her pink backpack and starting to pull her away.

"Wait! What's a robin?" she wanted to know. "Is it some kind of woodwind instrument? Or is this another one of those concepts that no one understands anymore?"

Mr. LaRue dropped his sticker book onto the concrete and glared at her. "You damn freaks!" he barked. "Trust you to take the pleasure out of spring!"

Cassie stepped behind her brother, and Martin allowed her to hold his hand. "*Damn*? I don't know what that word means," she whispered. "Martin, do you know?"

"It means time to go," he said. Then he hauled her away down the sidewalk.

"But what does it mean?" she asked again as they turned the corner and walked away from the park.

"It's just a bad word. It means you made him mad." She hadn't asked him about *freaks*, of course. She had learned that word long ago.

The suburb was laid out in concentric circles, like a dartboard. They crossed curving street after curving street of tidy brick houses with identical windows, doors, and garages. On each street, the color changed. All the houses were tan, or all pink, or mustard yellow. Martin passed them without seeing them.

Freaks, he thought. The word was as much a part of Cassie's life as the steel dome above them.

The ads had started running on mid-morning television the summer after Martin's fourth birthday. *WONDER BABIES are here!* they announced. *Be the first family on your block to raise a WONDER BABY!* Even as young as he was, Martin had been aware of Mom and Dad's interest. Mom had already talked about having another baby. Now Dad wanted one too.

Never had the arrival of the stork brought such excitement. Overflowing with charm, brimming with intelligence, Wonder Babies were like nothing the suburb had seen before. But that didn't turn out to be a good thing.

Wonder Babies didn't wait around to be raised. They got involved in their upbringing, wanted to know about their feeding schedules, and read voraciously before the age of two. Worst of all, Wonder Babies—or the Exponential Generation, as they preferred to be called—wouldn't stop asking embarrassing questions. No amount of time-outs, missed snacks, or spankings could break them of this awful habit.

Three years ago, when the first class of the Exponential Generation had reached kindergarten, their teacher had quit within the week. No one would stay in their classrooms and put up with the deluge of questions their bizarre genius produced. But that didn't matter. They were driven to learn. They went to school anyway, dividing up the duties and team-teaching themselves.

Martin eyed the thin little girl whom he was attempting to steer toward school. She was wearing a stretchy shorts set of bright magenta, accessorized with a purple sweater. She had donned one pink sock and one purple sock this morning with her white sneakers, and her wrists sparkled with various pieces of childish jewelry in rhinestone and plastic. Her blue eyes and short golden curls bobbing in every direction made Cassie look downright perfect, like a living doll—even he had to admit that. He couldn't understand how the neighbors could say such cruel things to her face. He knew how he could, of course, but that was different.

"This word list is so inadequate," Cassie said, typing away on her handheld. "It doesn't have *damn* or *robin*. What *is* a robin, anyway? Does anybody know?"

Martin hesitated. Granny had whispered things to him when he was very young, while they sat together in the bright, glorious wonderland park of his earliest memories. Granny had told him of small, quick creatures that whirred through the air like toy planes, creatures that were as soft to the touch as a handful of yarn. But Cassie couldn't keep a secret, and everyone knew the walls had ears.

"I dunno," he said. "Stop asking stuff or I'll tell Mom."

They reached the school beside the outermost ring of streets and joined their classmates on the noisy playground. Cassie went off to assemble with the other members of the Exponential Generation under the guidance of Jimmy, their eight-year-old leader. Martin threaded through the knots of students, looking around for his friends.

"Over here!"

Matt and David were waiting for him with almost identical grins. Matt immediately tried to grab him in a headlock. As they thrashed about, bumping into other students and raising cries of annoyance, Martin felt hands in his backpack.

"Let go of me, you doofus!"

He flung off Matt, who bounced against a larger classmate, received a smack to the head, and ricocheted back into Martin without losing a millimeter of his grin. Frowning, Martin turned away and set his backpack on the ground to examine its contents. Nothing was gone, but his handheld was flashing random patterns.

"You messed with this," he accused.

Matt was already overcome with glee, making noises like a badly tuned scooter, but David gazed up at him without a trace of guilt. "Uh-oh," he said. "Looks to me like your handheld has a bug."

"A bug . . ." Martin looked at the dancing lights for a few seconds, pressing combinations of buttons. Then he turned the handheld over, tweaked off the back cover, and studied the circuit board. There it was: an extra computer chip, colored bright purple. He pried it off, and the multipronged chip morphed in his hand. Now a small bug crawled across his palm, a purple bug with gold legs. David and Matt whooped in triumph and celebrated by punching each other.

"Sweet!" said Martin, examining the metallic computer bug. He put it back onto the circuit board so he could watch it freeze into chipdom and then pried it off again. "I wanted some, but my dad wouldn't buy them. He said they could damage the wrong kinds of machines."

"Nah," said David importantly, scooping up his chip. "These only work on little stuff—it says so right in the ad."

The bell rang, and the students squeezed into the main hall. The three friends allowed the force of moving bodies to carry them along.

"We put one on David's cat Cinder—gross! Shorted out the whole simulation."

"She turned into a big lump like silver Jell-O, and now she won't come near me. Here, I'll show you," David said. Chip in hand, he pushed through the crowd over to the Wonder Babies. Martin and Matt knew what was on his mind. Only one student brought a pet to school. Only one child answered to no one.

Jimmy stood at the door of the second-grade classroom, seeing the first group of Wonder Babies to its destination. He ticked off the roll on his handheld as children filed past him into the room. His pet rat, white with black patches, clung to his shoulder.

"Look out for a crash," David said, shaking the purple bug onto the rat.

The big piebald rat felt the bug crawl across its shoulder and scratched with its back paw. Then it seized the bug and sat up to sniff at it. Jimmy craned his neck to see and took the purple chip away. "I saw those on television," he remarked.

Staring, David took back his chip. Matt was punching him. "What happened, man?" Matt demanded in a whisper. David punched him back.

"You—man!" David stammered. "You—I mean, it—man! That thing's *real*!"

Jimmy walked his next group of charges to their room. Martin and his friends followed. "Hey, I want one too," Matt said in excitement. "Where do you buy a real rat?"

"You don't buy them," Jimmy answered. "I caught him in the warehouse area when he was a baby—Melanie, get rid of that gum."

"Can it change into anything?" asked Martin. "Like, different kinds of rats?"

"Or a rapid-fire slingshot?" suggested David, eyeing the long bare tail.

"No," Jimmy said. "He stays a rat. Brent and Margery, you start the reading lesson, and I'll be back in half an hour. Kindergarten Exponents, go to your room, and I'll be there to take roll in a minute."

Distracted from the rat, Martin speculated briefly on what it would be like to be eight years old and a teacher. Judging from the worried expression on Jimmy's face, it wasn't much fun.

"Look," Jimmy said as the little children filed by him, "Patches is alive. He was born, he grew up, and in another year, he'll die."

Death. Martin had a confused vision of a tiny black railcar coming to retrieve the furry body, just as one did when a person died. "Wow," he murmured. "That's very cool." He wondered about Granny's birds and clouds. Did they die too, like rats and people? How did that work?

"I'll buy one from you," Matt insisted.

"Yeah, we'll buy him," David said. "How much is he?"

Jimmy paused in the doorway, looking away from them.

He's disappointed in us, Martin thought. I wonder what we did.

"Rats," said Jimmy finally, "are *not* for sale." Then he shut the door.

"Stupid kid, stuck with a toy that can't do anything," David said, turning away.

"He made us late. Now we'll have extra work," Matt grumbled. "That stupid freak!"

Trailing behind them, Martin reluctantly entered his classroom. The sight of its familiar green walls crushed the happy thought of rats out of his mind. Pea green. Vomit green. A very appropriate color.

School was the usual interminable torment. In silence, the students worked exercises that had been fed into their handhelds, downloading the results to the school computer every half hour. In silence, Martin's teacher paced up and down, gazing out the window at the deserted playground. The computer had given him no lecture to read to them that day, so his only duty was to call time at the end of each exercise. But the handhelds did that anyway, a clock in the upper left-hand corner ticking down the time remaining before the termination of each drill.

Martin watched the seconds depart, scuffing his feet on the floor to provide a distraction. Across his screen paraded an endless succession of sentences to diagram, math problems to solve, science questions to answer, spelling errors to correct. When he daydreamed, the handheld beeped at him, and his teacher came over to shake him. By the end of the day, rigor mortis had set in, and his brain held no thoughts at all.

"It's your birthday," Cassie reminded him on the way home. "What present do you think you'll get?"

"I dunno," Martin said vaguely. He was still coming back to life.

"What do you want to get?" pursued Cassie, not for the first or even the tenth time that week.

"I dunno," Martin said again. "I guess Mom could give me back my jeans."

Cassie hooted. "Those old things! Everyone could see your underwear! I can't believe Mom had to sneak them out from under your pillow."

"I knew she was after them," Martin muttered. "They were just the way I like them."

"Oh, come on, what do you *want*?"

"Nothing, I guess." Martin was thirteen now, he reminded himself, not some dumb little kid anymore. Toys were for kids, and the things he was mildly interested in, like David's bug, he knew his parents wouldn't give him. But the sorts of things his father and mother gave to each other—puzzles, hobby kits, clothes, grown-up junk—he couldn't imagine ever wanting.

"You can't want nothing," insisted Cassie. She took his hand and tugged on it as she skipped and hopped in excitement. "There are so many things you don't have. Fun things! Pretty things too! I wish it were my birthday."

"That's just kid stuff, Cass," he said. "If you were old like me, you'd understand." And he stiffened his arm so she could hop higher.

Martin and Cassie reached the park. Crates and bags teetered in wobbly piles on the sidewalk in front of their house, and their father stood in the middle of the chaos outside their open garage.

Dad was comfortable-looking and a little soft, like his favorite recliner chair, with a cheerful face and a patch of long grizzled hairs that he carefully combed over his bald spot. Something was wrong today, though, Martin could tell. Dad's hairs were disarranged, and his movements were impatient. Maybe he and Mom had had a fight.

"You're home early," Martin said. "What's up?"

"I got the trash shipments out the door ahead of schedule," Dad said. "And the new scooter came in today. I thought I'd try it out."

Martin spotted Dad's new scooter leaning against the house behind a stack of Young Scientist in the Kitchen kits. Dad had been talking about his scooter for the last two weeks. He should look happier about its arrival.

"I can't even squeeze it in here." Dad gestured hopelessly

toward the garage. "I don't know why they didn't make these things with more storage space!"

"We could move the volleyball stuff," Martin suggested. "We never play. Or we could throw out Mom's old weights." Balancing several boxes of Cassie's baby clothes on top of the foosball table, they wedged the scooter in at last.

They burst into the dining room from the garage. Mom was there, hurrying from cooker to table. Mom always hurried, every movement decisive and efficient. She drank those hideous no-dye-added energy drinks all day, and they obviously worked.

"It's the birthday boy!" she cried, and Martin was subjected to a smothering hug and kiss. "I tried out my new cake-decorating module today. The frosting is 'a mystery flavor that will keep your company guessing for hours.' You'll have to tell me what you think."

As they ate their dinner and the enigmatic birthday cake, Martin kept an eye on his father. Dad didn't eat much, which was unusual. He didn't say much either, but that was typical. Cassie monopolized the conversation as always, telling them about her day.

"We finished *Peter Pan*," she said. "I thought it was well written, with vivid characterizations, even if the setting was a bit fantastical. Peter is a lawyer working for an agency that investigates companies for tax evasion. He takes on Captain Hook, CEO of the Jolly Roger shipping line, for failing to report stolen merchandise. With the help of the Lost Boys Accounting Firm, they finally get Captain Hook dead to rights." She paused long enough to take a drink of milk.

"My favorite character was Tinkerbell," she continued. "Tinkerbell works in advertising, so she can do magic. Captain Hook tried to make Peter Pan lose his job, so Tinkerbell ran a thirty-second spot on television about how great Peter was. That saved him, but then *she* was going to get fired. But then she said she thought she could keep her job if enough little children believed in advertising, and Peter Pan asked us to clap our hands if we did. And we clapped, and then she just got a verbal warning from her supervisor, and her biggest account was renewed for two more years."

"Reading *Peter Pan* in first grade!" said Mom, shaking her head. "And that's not what happened to Tinkerbell when *I* read it."

"What happened to your Tinkerbell, Mommy?" asked Cassie.

Mom shot her a stern glance. "Don't ask questions!"

This looked like the start of one of Mom's lectures, and those generally ended with Cassie running off in tears. Martin decided it was time for a diversion. "Great cake, Mom," he said. "I think it's banana. Anyway, something like that."

"My birthday boy!" Mom smiled at him. "You certainly are quiet tonight—you haven't said a word about presents. Not so long ago, you would have been begging to open your gift before the morning vote. Cassie, go get it for me." His sister trotted from the room.

Okay, this is the big moment, Martin told himself. Remember to look excited. Then a large object struck him in the chest, knocking his chair to the ground. Something heavy proceeded to dance on him. He gave it a shove and got a look at it. A big golden-coated collie was attacking him in a frenzy of affection, licking his face and yelping ecstatically.

Martin became aware of the sound of his own voice adding to the din. "STOP DOING THAT RIGHT NOW!"

The dog stopped whining and wriggling. Ears forward, it considered him. Then it flopped over onto its back and lay with its paws in the air, inviting him to rub its white tummy.

"'The Alldog,'" read Cassie from the side of a big cardboard box. "'Large or small, sleek or fuzzy—all the dogs you ever wanted rolled into one. Contents: one Alldog, owner's manual, and reset chip. Runs on two Everlite long-life rechargeable batteries. Batteries not included.'"

"He's all yours, son," Dad said, helping Martin to his feet. "They had us send in your photo and a dirty sock and programmed him right at the factory."

The collie, unable to contain itself any longer, flipped right side up and began swimming forward on its belly. When its nose rested on Martin's sneaker, it toppled sideways and began running in place. Its warm brown eyes never left his face for a second.

"'The Alldog,'" Cassie continued reading, "'is the perfect pet and particularly good with children. Do not place your Alldog in a strong magnetic field. Some assembly required.'"

This is just great, thought Martin. Here I am, thirteen years old, and Mom and Dad give me a dog. A dog! Everybody knows dogs are for little kids.

He thanked his parents for the degrading toy and took himself off to his bedroom. He was used to Cassie tagging along and invading his privacy. This time, the dog tagged along too. Martin turned on his light, tossed his school stuff onto the bed, turned on his plasma lamp, turned off the light so that the plasma lamp would show up better, and sank into his beanbag chair to consider his misfortune. The collie tried to join him in the beanbag, forcing him to retreat to his desk chair instead.

Since the plasma lamp didn't illuminate anything, but only brought an odd green and purple glow to the room, Cassie turned on the light again before she plopped down on his bed. "You aren't allowed in my room," Martin pointed out, but he was only observing formalities. At the moment, he wanted an audience.

"You don't like your birthday present," accused Cassie, tossing the Alldog box onto his pillow. The collie's ears lifted, and it raised its head from Martin's knee to fix him with a look of concern.

"I don't want some stupid toy," he said. "That thing's not real. Heck, it's not even a dog. It's just a circuit board attached to a big wad of silver Jell-O. Here, I'll show you. Give me that reset chip." And he got up to poke around in the box. The dog let out a sharp yelp and dove under the bed. By the time Martin had the chip, he couldn't find his pet.

"I don't see where it could have gone," he said, rummaging under the bed. "There's no room down here for something that big." After several fruitless minutes, he tried a different technique. "Dog, come!" he commanded, imitating his mother. "And I mean right now!"

A little cream-colored Chihuahua came crawling out from under the bed, whip tail curled between skinny legs. Its large ears lay against its round head like crumpled Kleenex, and tiny whimpers rose from it at every breath. Its enormous brown eyes practically held tears.

"Oh, how cute!" Cassie cried, and it immediately hopped onto the bed to take shelter with her. "Poor baby! Look, you scared it."

Martin watched the abject creature hide itself in his sister's arms. Then he flung the chip back into the box and reclaimed his beanbag chair. He felt even more annoyed for giving way to pity. David and Matt hadn't. They had reset David's cat.

"I'm not scaring anything," he grumbled. "Computer chips don't have feelings."

The Chihuahua jumped down and came slinking over to him, trying to make friends. "You look ridiculous," he told it. The little dog sat down in the middle of the floor, head hanging and sail-like ears splayed out sideways. It looked as if it had no friends left in the world.

Meanwhile, Cassie was at the box again, pulling out several pieces of Styrofoam in search of the owner's manual. Soon she was tapping buttons on it, bringing up the search screen.

"I think they do have feelings," she said. "Listen: 'The Alldog was developed out of a research project to make tool bots seem friendly. This innovative toy begins with a basic tool bot computer module, layered with an artificial intelligence engine. The AI engine, instructed in canine behavior, is ready to explore its environment with you. It wants to be a good dog. Your responses, as well as day-to-day situations, provide a unique learning environment. As the AI engine seeks success and attempts to avoid failure, it becomes a true individual. No other dog in the world will be like yours.'"

"That's good," Martin muttered. "Just look at the skinny little thing! Give me the—Whoa!"

The Chihuahua was expanding rapidly, like a dog-shaped

balloon. In a couple of seconds, a veritable monster lolled beside the beanbag, appearing to take up most of the bedroom. It stood up and towered over Martin.

"Look out!" he cried.

Cassie pressed keys and reviewed several pictures. "It's an Irish wolfhound," she told him. "That's what I'm saying: this computer *does* have feelings—sort of. It knows you're its master, and the AI part of it wants to succeed. Since you didn't like it as a little dog, it made itself into a big dog."

The wolfhound gazed quizzically down at Martin, its long tail waving gently. "No!" Martin said in what he hoped was a firm, masterful voice. "Bad dog for getting bigger than I am!"

The huge shape crumpled immediately, and the rough coat smoothed out to a satin gloss. In seconds, a trim, compact beagle stood where the massive wolfhound had been. It had a black back, a brown face, and four dazzling white feet. "Okay, that's better," Martin told it, and it danced with pleasure, its white-tipped tail slashing to and fro.

"Jimmy taught us about these tool bot engines," Cassie said. "They're pretty smart, but they're kind of simple at the same time. They have one or two big goals, and they dedicate all their resources to meeting those goals. We're more complicated in what we want to do."

Martin watched as the beagle sprang about, trying to attract his attention. "So all this thing wants is for me to like it?"

"'Loyalty to the master,'" read Cassie from the owner's manual, "'is the single trait common to every type of dog.' You're the master. It's programmed to want whatever you want."

"Sit!" Martin ordered the beagle, and it promptly obeyed. "Beg!

Roll over! Up! Down! Play dead!" Silky ears flapping, the little animal performed flawlessly. "Find the square root of sixty-four!" The beagle hesitated for a second and then jumped onto the bed to tap the keys of Martin's handheld.

"Look at that," Martin scoffed. "*Real* dogs don't do math!" And he headed to the bathroom with his latest game cartridge to find a little peace and quiet.

When he came back, Cassie was in her room. Supportive snatches of dialogue from her Tell Me About Your Day diary module drifted out from under her closed door. Martin turned and tiptoed down the hall. At this hour, his parents were usually discussing their day—or their children. Over the years, he had heard many things worth knowing. He stopped outside the living room, where a jewelry show was displaying the newest sparkles. Dad's voice was barely audible against it.

"I saw the first of them today, Tris," he said. "Coming off the packet from Central."

"The first whats?" Mom asked absently. *Your friends won't know it's not a zirconia,* the television assured her.

"You know! Just like last time. They'll be everywhere in a few days. I wish we knew what happened to—" He gave a sigh. "I just hope nothing turns up."

"Walt, what are you talking about?"

Martin heard the recliner creak as Dad shifted. "Inspection!" he hissed. "There, I said it. You had to make me say it!"

"Oh dear!" murmured Mom.

"Oh good, you mean," Dad said morosely. "You know the walls have ears."

CHAPTER TWO

Martin awoke to the stirring strains of patriotic music. At precisely seven o'clock, every television in the suburb had turned itself on and begun playing the national anthem. By a quarter after seven, families were expected to gather in front of those televisions to take part in the daily vote. No problem was too small for them to consider. They were an intensely democratic people.

"Those blue curtains look cheap, Walt," Mom was arguing that morning as Martin stumbled into the living room. "It's the Presidential Office. It should have dignity. He has to hold meetings in there."

"I like blue," Dad murmured sleepily. He was wearing his brown bathrobe, and the long strands of hair that he combed over his bald spot were flopping to and fro. He stood by the television, waiting for the input signal to come on. Then he pulled the keypad out from its shelf below the big screen and typed in his vote. Once it registered, he stepped back with a yawn. "Your turn, Tris," he said. "We'll cancel each other out like we always do."

Mom stepped forward with the brisk air of a woman who had her duty to perform and two cups of coffee inside her frame to help her do it properly. The national anthem never caught her in bed. She had already taken her shower and gotten dressed.

Voting finished, they waited to see the result. At seven thirty, the President came on-screen, handsome and serious, standing at a low podium in front of draped flags.

"Thank you, fellow citizens, for taking time out of your busy day to keep this great country running at its best," he said, looking so earnestly at them through the television screen that he seemed about to reach out and clasp their hands. "In entrusting these decisions to my people, I share with each of you the awesome burden of leadership. Your quick and caring response lets me know that I am not alone."

"He speaks so well," Mom whispered. "And he dresses so well! No one else looks that good in a suit."

"The people have chosen the dark green curtains with the yellow flecks—"

"Yes!" cried Mom.

"—and of course I bow to their will in this as in all else. Those of you who voted for the blue, take heart: your voice will prevail on another day. Be sure to watch this evening at six o'clock, when I present the problem for you to vote on tomorrow. Goodbye for now. As I guide our great nation, I will remember your faithful service."

The screen showed their flag waving proudly for a few sober seconds and then launched into a juice commercial: *Grapefruit never tasted so good!* Dismissed, they headed into the kitchen for breakfast.

"I don't understand voting," Cassie said as she took out her favorite cereal. "You never vote about anything big."

"That's good," Dad said, reaching for the coffeepot. "That means there's nothing big to worry about."

"But don't you ever get to vote for anything bigger than curtains or holidays? Like the President. I want to know when we vote for him."

"Don't be silly," Mom said, bringing dishes to the table. "Our President's perfectly good. We won't need to vote for a new one till this one wears out. Martin, no dogs in the kitchen." The beagle, which had been glued to Martin's side like an extra limb since he had awoken, reluctantly retreated to the doorway.

"But who counts the votes?" asked Cassie. "We don't even know." She stirred her cereal to make the milk change color. Martin poked expertly at his, causing alternate pockets of orange and blue dye to pool into the milk. Clinging to a cup of black coffee, Dad watched them without enthusiasm.

"Of course we know," Mom answered testily. "A big computer does the counting, right there in the room with the President."

"But we don't know that," observed Cassie. "We never see numbers for how many voted each way. The President could just decide which curtains he liked best and then say anything that—"

"*Cassie!*" cried Mom.

"Tris, I'll handle this," Dad said, and Mom snatched the milk from the table and went elsewhere. While his father talked, Martin watched his mother slam things around the kitchen. He couldn't believe Cassie had been dumb enough to talk badly about the President. These smart Wonder kids sure could act stupid sometimes. No wonder people called them freaks.

"You see," Dad said slowly, "the President would never tell a lie. He wouldn't do that because he's our leader. We don't talk about that kind of thing. Not ever. We don't even think about that kind of thing."

"Yes, sir," whispered Cassie.

"We don't talk disrespectfully about voting," he went on. "It's the most important thing we do. People who don't vote can't be trusted. When the time comes for job assignments to come over the computer, those people don't get jobs, and then they can't get married. They don't fit in anywhere, and no one wants to be around them. Sooner or later, they leave the suburb, and they don't come back."

I wonder where they go, thought Martin. Off and on, he'd become aware of certain people not in their houses anymore, of kids at school shrugging over someone on their block who had gone missing. But the suburb held several thousand residents, and the adults never mentioned the ones who had left.

"We're very lucky people," Dad continued, on familiar ground now. "Before, things were terrible: everybody getting sick, not enough food, not enough jobs. So they built the suburbs, and our families were the lucky ones who got to live here."

Martin was barely listening. Every lecture ended this way, like a little commercial. *We live in the suburbs, we're the lucky ones, we have everything we want.* Slurping cereal, Martin tried to imagine the alternative: sitting around outside the steel dome in the blowing waste of sand and poison gas that people said was out there.

"We have everything we want," Dad concluded. "We have an easy life. All the President wants in return is a little help, a little appreciation. That's not much to ask, now is it?"

Cassie shook her head, staring at her cereal as its colors slowly faded to gray. Martin gave her a little kick under the table. How many times had he warned her? If you want to find out about something, don't ask. It was much better to listen at doorways. And that reminded him.

"Hey, Dad, I want to come to work with you today."

Dad's eyelids flickered slightly. "Oh, I don't know," he replied. "Stuck in the loading bay when all your buddies are out having a good time . . ." He trailed off and looked appealingly at Martin.

Martin looked innocently back. "Come on, Dad, you always want me to go; you know, quality time and all. And now when I want to, you're backing off. What's the big problem?"

Dad swirled the lukewarm dregs of his coffee, stalling for time. If he raises an excuse, thought Martin, I'll just ask more questions. Pretty soon, it'll be obvious he's hiding something, and I know he doesn't want that.

His father must have come to the same conclusion. "All right," he said. "But I want you to promise you'll stay out of the way this morning. Big loads are coming in." He glanced at the clock. "Fifteen minutes till we leave."

Fifteen minutes was plenty of time to pull on the jeans that lay crumpled by Martin's bed and trade his pajama top for the T-shirt he'd worn to school the day before. So what if its logo had faded? It was the softest T-shirt he owned. But Mom would have a fit if she saw it two days in a row, so he prudently covered it up with a sweatshirt.

Martin shut the annoying little dog in his room, but before he got to the garage, it caught up with him again, giving shrill barks of joy at their reunion. That was strange. He walked back to Cassie's room. She was curled up on her bed with her big plush bunny and a coterie of sympathetic fashion dolls.

"Did you let the dog out?" he asked.

Eyes dull, Cassie shook her head, and Martin felt bad for her. "Do me a favor, stay out of Mom's way while I'm gone," he said, tugging a curl to watch it spring back into place. "Mom and Dad are freaked out about something, and I don't want to sit through any more boring lectures."

His tone was kinder than his words. Cassie gave him a grateful look. "Nobody let your dog out," she said. "I saw the door open by itself when I came down the hall."

Martin turned to the beagle, surprised and a little impressed. "Did you let yourself out? I didn't know toys could do that. I think that's kind of cool. Okay, computer dog, you can come with me."

Today was Sport Day, the first day of the weekend, and the streets reverberated with noisy life. Driving the scooter cautiously, Dad wove in and out of impromptu soccer matches, past a pickup basketball game going on around a streetside net, and through the middle of a freeze-tag tournament. Martin glanced back at the little dog trotting after them and began to see the fun of owning something that showed him such devotion. All the way across the suburb, its little paws pumped like pistons; but then, until its batteries ran down, that computer-chip creature never would get tired.

Dad turned down an alley behind the last row of buildings, where the steel dome, braced with its reinforcing network of girders, rose from its concrete bed. Here, it was not the tidy structure that appeared to float above them, but a heavy tangle of crossing I beams, ugly plates, and gigantic rivets, streaked with rust and bubbled with layers of thick powder blue paint. The nearest skylights—great flat butter-colored panels—were hazy with many thousands of lines and scratches. Martin squinted at them out of habit, looking for clues about the world outside.

Sometimes they glowed brightly, and sometimes they didn't, but he had never seen so much as a shadow move across their translucent surfaces.

"Get the elevator," Dad said. Martin jumped off the scooter, jogged to the tan door set in the back of the grocery store building, and typed his father's password onto the keypad. Martin had been getting the elevator for his father since he was old enough to punch buttons. Coming or going, Dad always seemed to have a vehicle to maneuver or an armful of stuff.

They rode the elevator down, which was the only direction it could go. At the bottom, they were in Dad's world.

Every day, as the suburbanites watched their television sets to alleviate their boredom with a sky that never changed, catchy ads alerted them to new products that they couldn't wait to buy. Shipments of goods arrived at the suburb constantly, and a steady stream of discarded items left. These were loaded into boxes, which were packed into larger boxes, which were put inside enormous boxes on flashing steel wheels, the packets that came and went on the rail lines. There was a packet for every need, from the refrigerated ones that held their food and the double-hulled ones that held the power plant fuel to the plain black packet that came when a local inhabitant died, the one that took a person to meet his maker.

Martin and Dad stepped out of the elevator into the loading bay, a large utilitarian space lit by banks of fluorescent tubes. Iron rails crossed and recrossed the polished concrete floor, and packets of all descriptions waited on those rails, in the process of being loaded via mechanical carts or overhead cranes. Yellow paint striped the floor, warning people where not to walk, but it didn't matter anymore. Only one human was on the payroll in the loading bay, and he didn't go near the rails. Tool bots did all the hard work these days.

Dad was the packet chief, in charge of making sure that the right loads were hooked up and waiting to leave on the rail lines. He sat at the computer console, reporting on arrivals and departures, as his freight bots assembled the packets, lined them up on the outbound rails, dragged in the arriving packets, and broke their contents down for distribution. Dad held the highest-paying job in the suburb: it required a reasonable amount of brains and attention to detail for a minimum of six days a week. Some people pitied Martin's father because he had to work for a living, but he said he enjoyed having something to do.

Dad tapped a key to bring up the computer screen, checking for the daily schedule. He typed:

SUBURB HM1 ONLINE GOOD MORNING FRED HOPE YOUR WEEK-END IS STARTING WELL

The bright green letters glowed at the output line for a few seconds, and then they moved up, replaced:

SUBURB BNBRX ONLINE GOOD MORNING WALTER THANK YOU FOR YOUR KIND WISHES BUT I PREFER NOT TO DISCUSS PERSONAL MATTERS

Dad sighed. "Fourteen years, and he hasn't unbent an inch. So much for the daily attempt at good manners."

The heavy-duty freight bots were clustering around now, ready for their orders, folded as small as they could be so that their many long telescoping arms would pose no danger to their boss. Dad began reading out the contents to be placed inside the first packet.

Martin scouted around the busy loading bay, looking for the mysterious "thems" that had come off the packet car from Central. A nudge at his knee interrupted him. The little hound was looking up at him, wagging its white-tipped tail. It, too, looked as if it were waiting for orders.

"No, I don't know what I'm after," he said irritably. "I'll know when I see it, though."

He skirted the large well-lit space, watching as the booms swung loaded crates into yawning containers. Several packets rolled by, screeching and thumping into one another as they slowed to a stop. A quick scan of them turned up nothing unusual.

The dog bumped Martin's knee again, its expression eager. Obviously, it counted on him to come up with some sort of plan. "I know what I'm doing," he told it. But he didn't. He stopped to think. "Okay, we'll see when the Central packet arrives today. Maybe more inspection things will be on it."

He sidled up to his father's console, trying to appear nonchalant. Dad's computer screen informed him that Central's shipment would come in at 8:57 a.m. Martin stepped back just in time to keep the beagle from nudging him again. "Look, computer chip, get your own life!" he snapped.

The dog's soulful brown eyes gazed up at him in unblinking adoration. *You are my life,* they seemed to say.

"Whatever," he muttered. "I guess we could kill time finding rats." His toy barked joyfully in agreement.

"Rats?" Dad said, overhearing them. "Son, we don't have rats in HM1." But Martin and the dog were already walking away.

Where had Jimmy found his rat? Martin remembered him

saying something about the warehouse. They followed a mechanical cart as it rolled down a short hallway and into a large high room filled with cardboard boxes resting on open shelves. The cart sprouted long stilts to deposit its load on a shelf above their heads, and they edged gingerly past it.

The beagle bounded ahead now, sniffing the cement floor. It led Martin into the produce room. Long flat boxes of fresh fruits and vegetables were stacked into chest-high towers by the door, and nectarines filled the shallow plastic bins of a rolling trolley nearby. Down the center of the room, specialized bots with many long rubber fingers were washing bunches of radishes at a white porcelain trough, and industrial refrigerators lined three walls, humming in a maddening whine.

The dog wove its way through the cardboard stacks, around the bases of the busy bots, and straight into a large mound of vegetable rubbish heaped against the unoccupied wall. By the time Martin reached the pile, it was digging furiously. Bruised lettuce leaves and dried-up orange rinds went flying through the air.

"Stop! Stop!" called Martin. "Get out of that junk!"

His dog emerged, tail wagging cheerfully. Moist brown apple peels clung to its nose and wound around its neck in a festive chain.

"You look gross," Martin told it severely. "Playing in the trash! Stop fooling around and get to work finding rats."

Shedding the peelings with a mysterious swiftness, the beagle sat down and yelped in protest, but Martin made it follow him back into the warehouse.

"Rats . . . ," he mused, looking down the aisles of cardboard boxes. At a loss, he studied the labels, as if one of the containers might be stamped RATS—SIX GROSS—STORE THIS SIDE UP—DO NOT OPEN WITH CUTTING TOOL.

The dog barked again, shrill and annoying. "Shut up!" Martin said. He glanced at his watch: 8:55. The packet was almost due.

Martin waited for the packet's arrival behind a load of new laundry-sorting machines, with a good view of the incoming rails but hidden from his father. Warning bells clanged as the large metal gates swung open, and the incoming packet rolled in dripping from the humid darkness of the washing room. No human had ever set foot in that room beyond the steel gates. Special machines there decontaminated the packets, so that the poisons couldn't come in from outside.

Just one car from Central today, its corrugated sides rust red. Martin scanned it, feeling disappointed. He didn't see anything strange. No, hold on. The little black box stuck on the under-carriage, right next to a big steel wheel. Had he seen one of those before?

As Martin walked forward to get a better look at the box, a panel on its side slid open, and water came pouring out. No, that wasn't right; it couldn't be water because it wasn't dripping. What liquid moved like that?

The silver substance clung to the bottom of the packet car, flowing along it with gluey sluggishness. A small wave formed, streaming down the big wheel, and puddled around Martin's shoes.

"Cripes!" he yelped, jumping back.

Hundreds of small oval forms were hurrying along, climbing over one another in their haste. They were fat and gelatinous, about an inch long, fringed by many short, rippling legs. As they surged across the wide space, they lost their silver color and mimicked the shiny gray of the cement floor. Within seconds, they disappeared, flawlessly camouflaged, their movement nothing more than a vague impression.

"Don't look at them," said a tense voice. Dad was behind him. "Act like you don't see them. We're not supposed to know about them, not really. Or be too nosy."

The mass of busy creatures made Martin shiver. He had the horrible feeling that one had glided up his sock. "What *are* they?" he asked, hopping on one foot to shake out his jeans leg.

Dad caught his elbow and dragged him away. "It's government business," he answered. "Don't ask about them. And don't tell. Remember, the walls have ears." He glanced uneasily at the invisible swarm. "Eyes, too," he muttered.

Martin followed his father to the computer console, still feeling as if those things were all over him. While Dad reported the arrival of the Central packet w/out incident, Martin rubbed the back of his neck to stop the tickles going up and down his spine. After a few minutes, the prickly feeling went away. "Come on, computer chip," he called to his dog.

"Where are you going?" Dad asked anxiously.

"Back to the warehouse," Martin lied. "We were hunting for rats."

Once they were out of sight behind the laundry machines again, he ducked down and studied the floor. Nothing moved there. The little horde was gone.

"Okay, computer dog, time to earn your batteries," he whispered. "Find me those crawly things." The beagle tilted its head and cocked one floppy ear in surprise. "Yeah, I know what I said to Dad. Just do what I tell you."

The dog obediently sniffed the floor, moving in the direction the shapes had gone. It trotted behind a stack of metal panels and followed a yellow-marked rail line out of the loading bay. A door slid open to let them through, and lights flickered on.

They were in a low room, octagonal and very wide, large enough to hold everyone in the suburb standing in a big crowd. The rail line bisected the space, but the warning stripes were gone; here, the floor was covered with dark gray vinyl embossed to look like stone. The brown paneling had an imitation wood grain pattern, and brassy fixtures held up flame-shaped electric bulbs with lights inside that wobbled back and forth.

This was the room where the black packet waited when one of the suburb's members died. Here, the people gathered, spoke about the deceased, and loaded up the body. Then, as they stood and watched, the packet car rolled off down the rails.

Martin could still remember the day when Granny had taken that trip. He had run after the packet, crying; in his memory, the rails were long bright smears. He had run all the way across the loading bay, following that big, scary box. Then the security horn had sounded its earsplitting blast, and a net of steel mesh had dropped down to catch him. The big gates had swung shut before he could struggle free. Granny had gotten away.

High-pitched yelping interrupted his reverie. The beagle was running in circles. It paused, whimpering, and looked around. Then it trotted toward a custodial bot that was vacuuming the floor nearby.

Bots came in all shapes and sizes. This one looked like a

small upturned trash can, ringed at the bottom by a circle of optical sensors. Its vacuum engine hummed away as it rolled repeatedly over a pale spot on the floor. Blocking its path, the beagle emitted a high, vibrating tone from somewhere inside its chest. The custodial bot switched off its vacuum and gave an answering whine, more tinny and even more annoying.

"Whoa! Computer dog, you speak bot!" Martin said, considerably impressed. "I've never seen a pet do that. Do the vacuum guy a favor then, and tell him that spot's gum."

Moving purposefully once more, the beagle trotted across the room and down a poorly lit hallway covered with old red carpeting that had raveled at the edges. Martin caught sight of a shimmer on the wall by his head. The trail of plump, glistening things was there, moving along steadily, blending in with the beige waffle-weave wallpaper. The creatures reached a door marked AUTHORIZED ENTRANCE ONLY and poured through a crack at the top of the doorframe. In a few seconds, they were gone.

Martin tried the handle. Locked. He fingered the keypad without hope. "Well, that figures," he said bitterly. "This place is all about locked doors, and no one ever does anything about it."

His dog studied the keypad, its brow wrinkled in thought. Then, slowly and carefully, it walked right up the door, its feet making plopping noises. It placed a paw over the keypad, and green numbers flickered across the screen. After a few seconds, Martin heard a click. He turned the knob, and the door swung inward, the beagle clinging to it like a stuntman. On the other side was vast darkness and the drone of machinery. "Unreal!" he whispered.

The beagle dropped from the door and trotted confidently

into the darkness, its eyes shining like flashlights. Martin still stood in the hallway. Maybe other pets could talk bot and light up their eyes, although he was starting to doubt it. What he knew without question was that no toy could unlock a door. His Alldog was malfunctioning. And this place—this big empty echoing blackness: he had never even heard about it before. It felt eerie, and it might be dangerous. He knew what he ought to do.

But as he hesitated, the beagle gave a shrill bark. *We're losing them!* the bark said. A rush of adrenaline jolted Martin, and he abandoned the safety of the hall. He heard the door lock behind him as he walked away.

The beagle's lighted eyes played over a network of conduits and ducts hugging the ceiling about fifteen feet above Martin's head. They walked past regularly spaced concrete pillars, enameled tanks, and square utility shafts. Then came an open area, interrupted here and there by more round, rough pillars. Then more tanks and shafts.

As they proceeded slowly, keeping pace with the movement of the weird things above them that only his toy could now see, Martin tried to place this huge, dim void in the context of the suburb he knew. Its rhythm was vaguely familiar. They must be in an access space beneath the houses. As the bot's lights danced faintly across the cement ceiling, waffled by thick support beams, he could distinguish a repeating pattern of pipes, tanks, utility shafts, and electrical lines matching each house. These curved away into the darkness as the houses curved along their streets.

They walked for a long time. How long, Martin didn't know. He couldn't read his watch in the dark. Mom had wanted to buy him a new watch with a glowing face, but Martin had preferred the old one. For the first time, he regretted his loyalty.

It was strange how noisy the place was and how silent at the same time. No sound could die away against the hard surfaces; it bounced around like a superball. The pipes overhead thumped and screeched, fluids boiled in the tanks, and off in the distance somewhere, the power plant's turbines hummed. Even the beagle's toenails made a decisive tap-tap on the pavement, high-pitched and steady, like a clock. It would seem that any more noise could hardly be noticed, but whenever Martin spoke, his voice was so loud that he felt the urge to talk in a whisper.

"Do you know how to get us out of here?" he asked.

The beagle, an indistinct shape in the darkness, didn't appear to answer. Martin could only hope that its tail was wagging reassuringly.

"And don't you think it's funny," he said later, "how much our steps echo? Mine sound like they're coming from everywhere. It's like there are a bunch of us down here."

An angry snarl interrupted him. The beagle was swelling in size. Its barks deepened from shrill to throaty, until a monster bayed savagely beside him, gnashing an impressive set of fangs.

Martin turned and ran into the darkness. Within seconds, he smacked into a pillar. The next thing he knew, he was sitting on the ground, and glowing lights were dazzling his eyes. A big wet tongue licked his stinging cheek.

"You're my dog, right?" he whispered, closing his eyes against the glare. He reached up and found himself petting shaggy fur. "You wouldn't . . . hurt me or anything, right?" He felt a long dog muzzle and two tall, pricked, velvety ears that folded beneath his touch. A big barrel chest vibrated as it whimpered.

"You're a good dog," he said shakily, fending off the moist tongue. "You're a good dog—a *big* dog! Man, you scared me!" He opened his eyes and squinted in the light. "Hey, shine those things somewhere else."

Bracing himself against the pillar, Martin slowly climbed to his feet. "Why did you change to another dog?" he wondered. "Don't do that again, it creeps me out. What were you barking for, anyway? O-o-oh, *crap*! There's something down here, isn't there?"

They ran all the way back, swerving around pillars and tanks. Martin kept his gaze fixed on his dog's bright eyebeams lighting up the concrete before him, afraid that the echoing clatter of his footsteps was the sound of a dozen monsters. A wall emerged from the darkness at last, and the dog directed them along it. In a few more seconds, Martin found himself standing in the hallway with the disreputable red rug, and the door closed and locked behind him with a gratifying click.

A handsome black-and-tan German shepherd stood beside him. "Wow! No wonder you sounded so mean," Martin said. "You're a tough-looking dog." The shepherd laid back its ears and wagged its bushy tail.

"Did you find any rats?" Dad asked when they walked into the loading bay. He looked up at Martin and whistled. "What happened to you? Did that rat take you out in twelve rounds?"

Martin examined his injured face in a shiny metal panel. A large, shallow abrasion puffed up the cheek. He thought it looked impressive.

"Nah, we didn't find any. I tripped over the dog." It barked in protest, and he gave it an apologetic pat.

"A German shepherd, eh?" Dad said. "Now, that's a good-looking brute." The dog nosed his hand, tail waving politely. "I'm glad you're back. I was thinking we'd go home for lunch a little early. Just let me get the 10:22 out the door."

Martin watched the freight bots closing up the packet car. He was still keyed up from his run. So many days were the same old thing, but today had been loaded with incident. An entire spooky world existed right here inside the regular one, and he wished very much that he could talk about it.

"Dad . . . ," he began. Don't ask questions, his mind advised. You went through a locked door that said AUTHORIZED, and he'll want to know how you did it.

Dad was typing out the contents list. "What, son?" he asked.

"Did you ever see a bot do something it wasn't supposed to?"

"Sure," Dad answered without looking up. "They break all the time."

"No, I mean something they're not supposed to be able to do. Like . . . like—oh, I don't know—like open a door by cracking the password."

Dad stopped typing and looked at him hard. "Have you seen this happen?"

"Oh! No, not really," Martin hedged. "It's just that—you know, even if I had . . . Anyway, David said he knew a bot that could."

"But you haven't seen it?" his father pursued earnestly. "You need to tell me. Yes or no."

Martin felt a cold nose against his hand. "No," he said, careful not to look at his dog. "I mean, you know—how could I?"

"Did David say he'd seen it?" Dad pressed.

"I dunno. Maybe," Martin said as casually as he could. "I mean, we're talking about David here. Why?"

Dad looked very serious. "Some bots are modified," he said. Alarm bells rang as the big gates swung open, and he typed a message on the console as the packet car slowly moved away. "We don't talk about it, but I think you should know so you can tell me if it comes up again. Modified bots can be very dangerous. Criminals buy them to be bodyguards, assassins—even bombs. Security notices come out from time to time, and we watch for them in the packets. Whenever you see a bot act unusual, you should report it for demolition."

Martin's dog was whining now. He stroked it reassuringly. "Yeah, but Dad, we don't know any criminals. How would a bot like that get in here?"

"Hopefully by accident," said his father. "They're made illegally in the factories, alongside the regular bots. Don't talk about this to your friends, but if David says anything else, I need you to tell me. Ready for lunch now? I'm going to take the new scooter around the outer ring to see how fast it'll go. Those things are supposed to do twenty miles an hour."

Now the shepherd was pawing at Martin, dark eyes anxious. "You know what, Dad?" he said. "I think I'll walk home."

On the way, Martin had a quiet talk with his dog. "You'll have to watch yourself," he advised. "If people are looking, just do toy things. And don't act so guilty all the time! It's lucky Dad didn't figure it out, the way you carried on in there." He ruffled the nervous dog's ears happily. "Man, you are one cool toy!"

As they passed tidy brick houses decorated with their yard

work stickers, Martin thought about the shadow world below. What a thrilling place it seemed once he was safely out of it! Its stark utilitarian spaces were almost irresistible. Now that he possessed an illegal supertoy that could take him into that prohibited zone, he would learn all its secrets and become master of its gloom. He imagined himself popping in and out of his friends' houses through a network of hidden doors.

But perhaps this underworld already had masters. Martin fingered his swollen cheek. If nobody else knew about the place, what exactly had his dog seen?

"Hold on! I know what's down there," he said in excitement. "It's the people who disappear!"

CHAPTER THREE

After lunch, Martin went back through the door marked AUTHO-RIZED ENTRANCE ONLY, but this time, he was prepared. He had armed himself with his Hi-beam flashlight/water cannon, but not because of the water cannon; it was the only flashlight he'd found that would still work. He'd loaded his backpack with an assortment of chocolate bars and sour bombs, his latest Hero Man comic modules, and (after some hesitation) a Women's Week module of his mother's, in the hope that such gifts would win him the gratitude and affection of any desperate under-world beings he might encounter. As he stepped out of the hallway with the hideous red carpet and followed his dog into the creepy space, he wished he could have brought Matt and David along for company. But neither of his friends could be trusted with a secret this big, and he didn't want them ratting on his dog.

"It's just you and me, computer chip," he said. "And hey, if you're a bodyguard bot, I'm gonna be just fine. Anyway, if you're a bomb, I don't think you'd blow me up. We're friends, right?" The shepherd wagged cheerfully.

They walked for a long time through the dusky concrete underworld that boomed and hummed with distant activity. The houses overhead clustered in tight rings as they approached the center. "Do you see any of them?" asked Martin, sweeping the shadows with his Hi-beam. "Can you find the people you saw last time?"

The shepherd nosed the cement floor. It wandered back and forth, sniffing, and then struck out in a straight line. Soon they came to a blank wall. The heavy door set into its surface was unlocked.

"Are they in here?" whispered Martin, worried at his plan's unexpected success. "Okay. I think you should go first." Light poured out as he opened the door, and the big shepherd walked through. Martin listened for ominous growls but heard nothing, so he stepped in and looked around, blinking.

The space was stylish, with polished black granite tiles on the walls and tasteful recessed lighting. But the area was designed not to attract attention. Like the plain gold band of a ring that served as the setting for a valuable stone, this space existed to display two impressive features. To Martin's right was a wide, clean, open flight of squared-off marble steps that came down from the street level of the suburb. To his left shone a sleek wall of clear glass, and through it, he could see the plush waiting room for a suite of executive offices.

An engraved brass plaque mounted on the wall of the lobby proclaimed the company name, but Martin didn't need to read it. "It's the factory!" he said. "But why would they keep anybody in here? Nobody works in the factory anymore."

The large factory had been busy in Granny's day, employing almost every adult in the suburb. Then had come the development of the independently operating tool bot. There had been a fear at first that they would mechanize the factory and lay off all the humans. Instead, employees had been given a choice: keep doing your job or lease a tool bot to do it for you. Regardless, they still earned a paycheck, spending it on the goods that kept their economy healthy. A robot could work, but it couldn't be a consumer.

At first, only the careful savers had been able to lease the expensive bots and feel the delightful thrill of not having to work. But soon tool bot prices had started to fall, and everyone could afford them. On-site management had continued for a while longer, but it became apparent that living managers weren't needed either. Strategic decisions had always been made at Central anyway, and the tool bots were model employees.

Everyone knew the factory was still there, churning out high-quality merchandise in some isolated area of the suburb. But no one walked through it anymore. It was every schoolchild's ambition to earn mediocre scores and qualify for a factory job. Then they could sit at home all day and get paid to watch television.

Martin crossed the lobby to the attractive waiting room. Heavy glass doors slid open, and he stepped onto the thick pile of a cream-colored rug. He expected the place to be dusty and run-down, but soft music played over the hidden speakers, and everything sparkled. The receptionist might have stepped down the hall for five minutes instead of fifty years.

"Custodial bots," he said as the shepherd joined him. "Those guys don't have the sense to stop polishing."

They walked through the managers' suite and found the rooms empty and bare. Only one office seemed odd. In the middle of the handsome mahogany desk stood a large, airy sculpture. On closer inspection, it turned out to be chicken bones, bleached and glued together. Martin's dog sniffed it and growled softly.

"I bet one of the disappeared people made it," said Martin. "They must have a lot of free time. Hey, you don't think anybody has died down here, do you? I wouldn't want to find anybody lying in a corner or something."

They wandered the industrial hallways, looking into a deserted laboratory and a records room full of old computer consoles. "Let's see what we make," Martin proposed, heading toward the racket of the workshops. "I've always wondered what we export. Maybe it's something cool, like power plant fuel, except I never see any of those fuel containers leave the loading bay unless they're empty."

The taupe fabric panels of the hallway blunted the noise considerably, so Martin was surprised at the din when he pushed open a swinging door.

"What a mess!"

The big rectangular room held thirty or forty workers knitting at brightly colored projects. The tool bots were stuck everywhere to the walls and ceiling, all their metal pairs of arms flashing busily, like big spiders with too many legs. The floor and table space that they had vacated was taken over by massive wads of loose yarn—vibrant red, bright blue, butter yellow, jewel-toned purple—so deep that no one could have waded through them. Many long lines of that vivid yarn fed from the piles to the untiring bots above them, forming a colorful web that could trap a person foolish enough to stroll through.

As the bots completed their knitting projects, they dropped them into a system of tubes that ran around the edge of the room. Martin walked down the hall to the next room and pushed open another door to see where the tubes led. Here, the room was heaped high with soft drifts of fabric stuffing, and bots were filling the knitted shells and tossing them into waiting bins.

"We make *bears*? This whole suburb is here for the stuffed bear market? That's gross! I'm not looking in the other workshops. They probably manufacture toilet paper!"

The shepherd stopped abruptly. Then it pointed its long muzzle up at the taupe-colored wall and gave a low howl. Martin came to investigate and noticed a flicker at eye level. A solitary oval form was moving along, its perimeter of hairlike legs undulating in a continuous wave and its fat body gleaming smoothly, like beige plasticine.

"It's one of those inspection things!"

Martin watched as it crawled for a few feet. Then it flattened itself briefly. When it moved on, a pearly cylinder was sticking to the wall where it had been. The tiny object protruded a few millimeters, round end facing out, about the size of a sequin. Martin tapped it cautiously. It felt like it might be glass.

Walking down the corridor, he found more of the little cylinders clinging to the wall, glistening wetly, like the whites of tiny eyeballs. Spaced about ten feet apart, the minuscule things were all but invisible until he knew where to look.

"Government business," Martin told his dog. "Maybe they have something to do with the disappeared people. Where are those people, anyway? I thought you knew where they went."

The shepherd recommenced sniffing, wandering up and down. It led Martin through a series of passageways and past more noisy workrooms, then stopped, growling quietly.

The narrow room before them held a kitchen cabinet complete with cooker and refrigerator, a couple of sofas, and a long dark brown vinyl-topped table surrounded by padded dinette chairs. A large television set was blaring away in the corner. The managers' break room still looked comfortable, even after fifty years of no management.

A bearded man sat at the table across from the television. He had far too much hair, a long russet mane of hair, and his beard started high on his cheeks and engulfed the lower half of his face like a fuzzy brown fungus. Only a bit of pale skin around the eyes and his high-bridged nose managed to escape the scrubby growth. He was wearing a worker's uniform of pale blue cotton and carrying on a running dialogue with the talk show host, a kind of counterpoint to the woman's comments. His brown eyes, lively and shy, slid by Martin in the doorway. Martin's presence appeared to affect the content of his speech, but not its fluency.

"It's played by colors," he said, speaking with a bit of a quaver, and Martin noticed the mounds of metal disks that lay on the table before him. "Each disk has a color dot, and I have to set them up in sequences. If a stack falls over, I lose. If I get to twenty, I win. Want to know what I win? Nothing. Want to know what I lose? Nothing. That's the nice thing about this game." He held the disks delicately in long fingers, but his fingernails were ugly square things, bitten down to the quick.

Martin took a cautious step into the room and leaned against the refrigerator to steady himself. He and David hatched plans all the time, but they never came to anything. The astounding success of this one had left him dizzy.

"You're one of the disappeared people, aren't you?"

"I saw you out there," the man remarked, waving a long white arm toward the wall. "You and your toy. Your Alldog. Good boy," he said to the German shepherd, who had positioned itself between them. The dog gave a low, rumbling growl. The man grinned, his teeth a white surprise in that dark woolly growth. "Stupid jerk," he said in a friendly way.

It took Martin a few seconds to realize that the stranger hadn't answered his question. He drew in a breath and tried again. "Where are the others?"

"Up there." Now the long arm waved toward the ceiling. "Up where there's law and order. Beer and skittles. Mom and apple pie. Plum Street, a cozy little bungalow built for two. There were three of us, though." He laughed in a nervous falsetto. "I guess that was the problem."

"I remember you," Martin said slowly, thinking hard. Sometime past—maybe two years ago—a good-looking student had vanished shortly after failing the eleventh grade. His outrageous stunts had made him popular, and his classmates had missed him. This hairy creature didn't look like Martin's mental image of the cocky young student, but Martin saw a bit of resemblance as those shy brown eyes glanced at him.

"Wanna know my name? It's Bug," the creature said eagerly. "Why? Because I'm the Bug in this program. Get it? Every machine has a Bug. This machine has a Bug. Great, huh? *I* like it."

"I thought your name was James, Gerald, something like that," Martin said. "What did your parents call you?"

"Who! Gives! A! *Damn!*" cried Bug, pounding his fists on the table. The little stacks erupted, and the metal tokens danced about. He stared in surprise at his clenched fists, at the ruin of his solitaire game. Then he started sorting disks once more.

The shepherd was growling again, a nasty sound deep in its chest, and the hair on its neck and back stood up in a ridge.

Martin tried to pat the hair down, wondering what to do. This guy was crazy, and not just crazy the way Matt and David said *crazy* to each other. Maybe he was dangerous.

"I wasn't what they wanted," Bug was saying to himself, as if he had forgotten about Martin. "Never what they wanted. They paid good money too. I should have come with a guarantee. I didn't go for that moronic voting, that stupid school, those stupid teachers. They warned me, so I broke into the loading bay and put stuff by the big doors, like I'd gotten out. Then I took Granddad's badge and hid here. And nobody ever found me."

Martin recalled fragments of a mysterious conversation from that time, noteworthy because his father's voice had been so angry: *No way to tell what happened . . . Left in my loading bay! . . . Of* course *there are alarms, but if the freight bots didn't weigh it properly . . . No, I am* not *going to file a report. Can't you see they'd blame* me*!*

"My dad thought you did get out," he said.

"Nobody ever found me," continued Bug, as if he hadn't heard. "Nobody ever looked for me. Nobody cared where I went. Know why? 'Cause I'm nobody."

"Are the rest of you down here too?" asked Martin.

Bug rapidly stacked disks. "No rest for the weary," he said. "Nobody's ever here, just me and the television. Now nobody, television, boy, and dog. Uh-oh!" He looked troubled. "What if I'm seeing things?"

"But where are the others?" Martin asked again, raising his voice. "There's more, right? I mean, you're not the only one who's disappeared."

"Disappeareds don't disappear here," said Bug. "Disappeareds

disappear out of here. Just like what would have happened to me."
His tower of disks fell over at last, and Bug continued in a quiet
singsong, "Just me, you see—nobody looks after me but me."

"You mean you had the chance to go somewhere else? Man,
that would have been really cool! I think you should have gone."

Bug stopped his game. "You know what you are?" he said
with menace. "You're a moron, that's what you are! You're too
stupid to be real. I *am* seeing things. I bet I could wave my hand
right through you."

He stood up, and Martin took a step backward. "Hey, you know,
I've gotta go now," he said in what he hoped was a casual tone.
"I've got stuff to do. Dad's probably wondering where I am."

"Your *dad*!" Bug crashed his fists down on the table again, and
Martin and the little disks jumped. "Your *dad* was a test tube!
And your *mom* was a petri dish! You don't have a birthday—you
have a sale date!"

This was too much for Martin's dog. The big shepherd leapt
over the table and pounced on Bug, toppling him over and out of
sight. Disks went flying in all directions with a crash like a slot
machine jackpot. Martin raced around the table to find the man
pinned to the ground. He was gurgling hysterically, and his eyes
looked as if they might pop out of his head.

"Hey, computer chip, let go!" called Martin, trying to pull off
the snarling shepherd. It released Bug, but he didn't get up. He
lay among overturned chairs, clutching his arm and rocking
from side to side.

Martin dragged the dog around the table. "Look," he said,
"you've gotta not go attacking people! I know maybe you're a
bodyguard, but you'll have to guard some other way. Unless

someone's trying to kill me or something, no snarling and biting! Toys don't bite! Bad dog! Got that?"

Ears flat against its head, the shepherd wagged ingratiatingly and tried to apologize by licking Martin in the eye. Martin discovered that he was shaking. He picked up an overturned chair and sat down in it.

"I'm really sorry about that," he said in the direction of the fallen man. "My dog didn't mean to hurt you, he just didn't know any better. Hey, you want some candy?" he asked, remembering the gifts he had brought. He dug into his backpack. "You can have a chocolate bar."

Standing up in stages, as if he were trying a yoga exercise, Bug reached out for the peace offering. "Chocolate!" he said feebly, collapsing into a chair and peeling back the wrapper. "The break room cooker won't make desserts. It's always lunchtime and never dessert." He ate the bar slowly, stopping every now and then to finger his bruised arm. "The bar's real, anyway. But that toy can't be real."

"Well, my chip dog's real, but he came from the factory with—I don't know—a different set of chips." Feeling in need of moral support, Martin unwrapped a chocolate bar of his own. "We were following these crawly government things, so he unlocked a door and let me in down here. That's how we found you."

Bug had been licking chocolate off the wrapper. He stopped and crumpled it in his hand. "What government things?" he asked quietly, as if he didn't want to hear the answer.

"Oh, sorry!" said Martin. "I forgot. I'm not supposed to talk about them. I really shouldn't be talking about my dog, either, but I guess you know about him already."

The strange young man drew himself up to glare at Martin. Then he glanced at the watchful shepherd and buried his face in his hands instead. "Look, my life has been hard enough down here," his muffled voice pleaded. "And this is all very weird. Weird, feared, jeered, beard. Weird. Disappeared-weird. Don't make it any weirder than it already is."

Martin ate the chocolate piece by piece, considering what to do. "Come look, then," he said, standing up.

Out in the hallway, Bug examined the line of sequinlike glass dots, uttering a fluent and colorful stream of expletives. Sometimes they rhymed, and sometimes they crackled in syncopation, like irregular machine-gun fire. Many of them sounded as if he had made them up on the spot.

"No more nobody for me," he concluded grimly. "I'm not the Bug anymore. These are bugs—*real* bugs! Looking, listening bugs. They're damn well going to find me now. I'll be disappeared for sure."

"Well, that might be kind of cool," Martin said. "I mean, getting to leave and all."

Bug jerked around to face him, and Martin's excited dog had to turn a snarl into a sneeze.

"Idiot!" Bug snapped. "They'll put me on the shows! That's what they do with the disappeareds. You did something wrong, so you play till you die, and everybody out there watches. Little kids spill popcorn in the sofa cracks while you go down for the last time."

"You're crazy!" Martin said. "Nobody dies. You can't show stuff like that on television. People get on the shows to win things."

"Win?" Bug tried to scrape off one of the dots with a bitten fingernail. "Did you ever see them win?"

Martin tried to remember. Mom didn't let him watch the shows, so he hadn't seen much. "They're too greedy," he said slowly. "They always want to keep playing."

Bug was breathing hard. "When do they say that? Huh? Never! The host says it for them. 'He's decided to keep playing.' But they don't *look* like they want to keep playing. Winners! There's no winners. There's only losers. Sooner or later, they all slip up, and then it's *into* the snake pit, *off* the rock wall, *under* the gas, and while the girls carry his body out, let's tell the people what he would have won!"

Martin had a horrible image in his mind of the old man on the show Cassie liked. That old man had looked like . . . well, he had looked like something was wrong.

"You have to get me out of here," Bug said. "You've got to help me!"

Martin shook his head. "Hey, wait, this is your problem. I can't do anything about it, I'm just a kid."

"It's your problem now. Yours and mine. Ours! You found me, you found the problem, so you gotta help me think. Think! *Think!*" Bug lurched toward Martin, hands outstretched and eyes wild, like a late-night-movie monster.

Martin ducked away and bumped into the wall. "Look, I'm sorry I bothered you," he heard himself babbling. "I think I better go now. Computer chip, you know, what I said before, I think I was wrong about biting."

The shepherd, positioned between the two of them, didn't know what to do. It danced with worry, alternately growling and whining. Bug tried to soothe the dog with a reassuring smile, but the expression that crossed his face was more frightening than ever—a kind of ghastly grimace.

"No, don't bite me," he bleated. "Don't eat me, you attack bot! You modified, oddified, unlockified bot." His brown eyes lit up. "Wait, that's it! That's the answer! Your bot can unlock doors. He can unlock the steel gates!"

"Hey, yeah, that's kind of crazy," Martin said, backing away, "but, you know, it's something to think about. So, tell you what, we'll think about it, and we'll, you know, we'll be in touch. Which way out of here?" he asked his dog.

Bug followed him down the hall. "That modified bot, he's illegal, right? If you don't help me, I'll report you."

"You would not!" Martin said. "You wouldn't report me because they'd find you. You said you don't want them to find you!"

"Like I've got anything to lose," answered Bug with a manic grin. "I've been a loser for a long time. You're the one with a life. You meet me in the alley above the loading bay tonight, or I'll turn in your dog tomorrow. Hiding a modified bot, that's a criminal offense. Watch out, kid, or they'll put *you* on the shows."

"Just leave me out of your sick problems!" shouted Martin. He turned a corner and started running.

"Be there!" called Bug's voice behind him. "Or your bot's not gonna be modified for long!"

CHAPTER FOUR

Dad was just signing off the computer console when Martin got back to the loading bay. "The new bowling balls came in," he said. "I picked out a red one for your mother."

Dizzy and out of breath, Martin didn't comment. He watched the freight bots towing the last of the packets away from the big steel gates. Outside, he thought. He wondered how bad it was out there.

"Martin, are you listening? Get the elevator button! This thing is heavy."

Martin rode home on Dad's scooter, thinking no coherent thoughts at all. When the scooter pulled up at the house, he climbed off and headed straight for the door. David and Matt had to chase after him, yelling.

"Where've you been?" David panted. "Never mind. Let's go! We're taking apart Matt's Devil Dominator game and putting the bad guys into my ImCity cartridge so they can blow up all the cute little houses. We've got this one zombie on the trolley already, shooting everybody who tries to go to the restaurants."

"He's so cool!" Matt said.

"Shut up," David told him. "Anyway, now we need your help. We can't get the slime demons out right. They show up as rainbow-colored puddles and won't suck people in and dissolve them. I can't figure it out, and Matt's useless."

"Yeah!" Matt said.

Martin didn't answer. They stood looking at him expectantly, and he stood staring into space.

"What's wrong with you, anyway?" David asked.

"I dunno," Martin said. Then he went inside. The doorbell rang furiously, but he ignored it.

Cassie was sitting on the floor watching television, with a glass of purple juice on the table nearby and a bag of onion squares in her lap. Martin threw himself down on the couch and closed his eyes. His shepherd jumped up beside him.

"Somebody's at the door," Cassie said over the noisy ringing of the bell.

"Yeah," he sighed.

"Aren't you going to get it?"

"They'll stop," he said, and shortly afterward, they did. Encouraged by this, he leaned forward to swipe her onion squares and glanced at the television screen. The weary face of Dr. Rudolph Church looked out at him.

"Cassie!" he shouted. "No!"

"I get to pick, I was here first," Cassie said. "We watched what you wanted last time. And Mom doesn't care because she's not here right now. She's still at her judo lesson."

Martin stared at the haggard old man behind the gleaming silver podium. There was a look in Dr. Church's eyes that made him ill.

"He's just beaten the highest score!" Cassie said excitedly. "He's won the biggest prize ever, and can you believe it? He's still going to play!"

"Did he say that?" asked Martin. "Did you actually hear him say that?" A bead of sweat trickled down Dr. Church's face, and

Martin knew the truth. "Of course not," he murmured, feeling the sweat break out on his own face. "The host said it for him."

And now, for thirty-five thousand dollars and ten cases of Au Gratin in a Box: What ingredient gives the popular bouncy toy FlyBall its amazing spring?

Martin didn't know. He felt a flurry of panic and found himself hating the smiling host. "So what happens on this show if you don't know the answer?"

"It's called *You've Been Caught Napping*," Cassie said. "Get it? You fall asleep."

No, you don't, Martin thought. You fall down dead.

Chad, that would be the insect-derived protein, resilin.

Cassie clapped along with the studio audience. "Isn't he amazing?" she gushed. "All the Exponents are watching him because he's the only grown-up we know who's like us. He's like"—she paused for inspiration—"like our dad!"

Hear that gong? Dr. Church has earned the chance to compete in our double-dozen sweepstakes. And guess what, viewers? He's decided to play!

Dr. Church seemed to be staring at Martin right through the screen, as if he blamed him for not doing something to help. *You're just going to sit there, eating your sister's onion squares. You're just going to watch me die.*

Martin snatched the remote off the end table, and the room roared with the din of motor scooters.

"You're mean!" cried Cassie, jumping up. "You know I want to watch that!"

"It's sick, Cass," he said bitterly. "Watch it again and I'll tell Mom."

Cassie stormed out of the room as noisily as a small, skinny girl could manage and slammed her bedroom door hard enough to rattle pictures on the walls. Once she was gone, Martin knelt down by the television screen and flipped through the afternoon game shows. Here was *Laserbattle,* a misty stage where black-suited gladiators hid behind boulders, shooting each other with red beams. Martin had to admit, it looked like fun. But then a pudgy woman stood up to fire, and red light struck the medallion on her chest. She fell to the ground, and Martin's stomach flipped over. He could tell she wouldn't be getting back up.

Next was *Obstacle Course,* a sleek gray-walled maze. Three men were scrambling over rope walls and trying to avoid trip wires. The ground gave way beneath one of them, a hidden trap yawning into blackness. Clawing at the edge in a desperate frenzy, the man slid into the pit.

"Change the channel, Martin."

Mom was back, still wearing her loose white judo gi, her long hair tied up in a ponytail. Martin stumbled over to her and let himself be held, as if he were a much younger boy.

"Mom, those people!" he groaned. He closed his eyes, and the man was sliding into the pit again. Mom led him into the kitchen and poured him a soda. His shepherd nosed him, whimpering softly.

"Those people are criminals," Mom said, pouring herself some tomato juice. "They're getting what they deserve."

Martin rubbed his forehead to try to press out the images. "But even for criminals!"

"If we knew what those people had done, we'd probably cheer. I won't say it again: dogs out of the kitchen." The shepherd retired to the doorway. "But we don't have to watch them," she went on, leaning across the table to ruffle his hair. "I know how you feel. I don't like to see it either. Sometimes it's better to turn your back on things."

"Sure, Mom," he sighed. Criminals, he thought, feeling a little better. Maybe that old guy of Cassie's had done awful stuff—killed babies or something.

"Now, what happened to your face?" Mom asked, and the scrape on his cheek smarted as she touched it. "Has my boy been fighting again?"

"No," Martin said. "Just wasn't looking where I was going."

When Cassie heard Martin come down the hall a few minutes later, she opened her door. He expected her to be mad at him, but she wasn't. "Mom came in just after I left," she said in a low voice. "If you hadn't made me stop watching that show, I'd be in trouble!" Good old Cassie, always convinced that her big brother was looking out for her.

"Why do all your dolls have those same big spooky smiles?" he muttered, wandering into her room. He sank down onto the thick purple carpet, and his dog snuggled up beside him.

"You poor baby," Cassie crooned, sitting down to pet it. "You're stuck with my nasty old brother! If he's mean to you, you can come and be my dog. What's his name?" she wanted to know, and the shepherd looked up, dark eyes alert. Apparently, it wanted to know too.

"I've kind of settled on Chip," Martin said. "You know, because of his computer chips." Chip's tail thrashed wildly in approval.

"Chip. Chip." Cassie rolled the name around in her mouth as if she were trying out a new flavor of ice cream. "I don't know.

He's so beautiful, and Chip seems too plain. I'd name him something like Ravenhair or Stoutheart."

"That's so fairy-tale!" Martin scoffed. "Chip's a dog, not a knight in some dumb after-school special. See, he likes 'Chip,' don't you, boy?"

The shepherd licked his face and tried to climb into his lap. Martin grabbed his legs and tipped him over, then joined him in a wrestling match.

"Last night, it was 'That dumb toy,'" Cassie said. "Now you're giving him hugs. Mom said you would. You never like things till you've had them for a while."

The doorbell rang, and Martin attempted to rise. "It's Matt and David. I need to go."

But it wasn't his friends. Baby wails came down the hall, and an angelic-looking toddler appeared in Cassie's doorway. She wore a blue velvet dress, shiny black shoes, and a big sparkly bow in her hair. At the moment, her face was beet red, and her nose was running like a faucet.

"I can't stand it anymore!" she bawled. "I can't put up with this for another minute!" And from the sound of the voices in the living room, it seemed her mother felt the same way.

"Look, Laura," coaxed Cassie, pulling the toddler onto her lap. "Look at the beautiful German shepherd! If you study his coat, you'll find red, beige, brown, and black hairs all intermixed. But from a few feet away, your eyes ignore the exceptions and see only the main colors. That's why he's called a 'black and tan.'"

Chip wore a patient expression as Laura sobbed into his fur. She calmed down after a minute or two and parted his coat to look at the hairs. "You're right," she sniffed as Cassie mopped her face with a tissue. "And the hairs are in a pretty pattern. How do they know to grow like that?"

"This fur doesn't grow," Cassie replied. "It's just a simulation. But on a real German shepherd dog, hair growth is controlled by genetics."

It's like these kids are in school all the time, Martin thought in disgust. He got up and left the room, taking the genetics exhibit with him. Freaks, he thought without meaning to.

"She's not like a baby at all," Laura's mother was lamenting in the living room. "I hold her on my lap, and she wants to talk about why skin wrinkles when you age. I worked so hard to plan her room, and she won't touch her toys. I wouldn't give her a handheld, so she used her chocolate pudding today to write division problems on the wall!"

"Laura's a Wonder Baby, Monique," Mom pointed out with a sigh.

"It's not fair!" Monique wailed. "I wanted a regular baby! I didn't want one of these fancy models. Why can't the stork bring us regular babies anymore?"

"Mom, I'm going over to David's," Martin called, heading out the door. Slime demons—that was what he needed! Yes, he desperately needed slime demons to bring the day back under control.

That night, Martin lay in bed and watched the bright numbers on his clock count up toward midnight. Bug wouldn't do it, he thought. Bug wouldn't turn Chip in and get Martin in trouble. It was a stupid plan. And even if he did, it wouldn't matter because Martin was just a kid. Kids weren't criminals; everybody knew that. No one would put Martin on the game shows.

The game shows! Images filled his mind: the pudgy woman falling, the man sliding into the pit. *What ingredient gives the popular bouncy toy FlyBall its amazing spring?* Who would even know that kind of thing?

And what about Chip? *Whenever you see a bot act unusual, you should report it for demolition.* That settled it. Martin wasn't about to let somebody demolish his dog.

"Come on, Chip," he whispered as he sat up and reached for his sneakers. "We better go take care of this."

In the middle of the night, the alley above the loading bay was as dark and creepy as the suburb's underworld had been. The dome's faintly glowing skylights seemed to hang in the blackness overhead like incandescent slabs suspended in an eerie void. Martin had to take out his Hi-beam to key in his father's password.

"Hurry up!" Bug hissed in his ear.

They rode the elevator down to the loading bay, and Martin turned on the fluorescent lights. He had thought he would feel better down here, but he didn't. Instead, he felt the vague unease that comes from being in familiar surroundings at the wrong time of day. Nothing about the brightly lit room seemed to have changed, but something was out of place. That something was Martin, standing in the loading bay in his pajamas. He belonged in bed.

The freight bots, with their strange and powerful steel shapes, came out of the corners. Chip spoke to them in his vibrating tool bot hum, and they drew back. There was no need to be scared of them, Martin told himself; he'd practically grown up with these bots. But tonight they seemed different. He didn't want to turn his back on them.

Bug made things worse. He was in a state of panic. "Okay, let's go!" he shouted. "Out of here! Now! Wow! Pow! Get those doors open!"

"Look, I think you should think about this," Martin said. "I mean, you shouldn't just walk out there. It's nothing but sand, and you ought to have a bag or something over your face for the poison, and anyway, you don't even have any stuff to take with you."

Bug walked down the rails a few feet, bouncing on his toes and swinging his arms like a runner before a race. "Kid, we both know I'm gonna die out there," he said. "And you're telling me I need to pack?"

Chip seemed to be acting unusual. He no longer fawned on Martin and looked for petting and guidance. Instead, he surveyed the packet rails and held a humming conversation with one of the bots. For the moment at least, it seemed as if Chip had forgotten to be a dog.

"Look," Martin said to him in a low voice, "I want you to take Bug outside if you can, but don't let anything happen to you. I don't want you getting caught by some alarm and getting sent back to Central for demolition. I'm sorry, I think he's nuts for doing this, but whatever, if it makes him leave us alone. Just be sure you stay safe. I'm gonna worry till you get back."

Trotting between the rails, Chip led the way to the steel gates. About ten feet from them, he froze and glanced back at Martin. Martin turned to Bug.

"Okay, this is it," he said. "Here's my flashlight. It's got water in the cannon part in case you need something to drink."

He tried to give it to Bug, but Bug wouldn't take it. He was staring past Martin without moving, as if he had turned to concrete. Martin looked around to see why. "Holy moly!" he breathed.

A very odd-looking packet car now stood on the rails, waiting for the gates to open. It was about two feet high and flat on top, like a rolling table, but this "table" had a German shepherd's black saddle spread out as a design across its surface, and its square legs faded to tan. A stylized tail of sorts hung down from the back, and Chip's head poked out the front. The head, panting slightly, looked perfectly normal, as if it didn't realize its body was gone.

Martin felt the hairs rise on the back of his neck. He had to swallow before he could speak. "I think," he whispered to Bug, "that he needs you to ride out. You know, so you won't set off the air horn."

Bug walked over to the dog-car in a kind of dream. He had a strange look on his face, as if he no longer saw or heard anything. He sat down gingerly, crossing his long legs, and the car gave a lurch and started to roll.

"Good luck," said Martin. Too late, he realized he had whispered.

The gates swung wide, dwarfing the miniature packet, and the crazy-looking pair rolled through. Martin cringed, expecting the earsplitting horn to go off, but they rolled into the washing room without incident, as his father would have said. After a few seconds, the gates swung shut again, and he was left alone.

He sat down on the cement floor and waited. The loading bay was very still. The multiarmed freight bots had stopped right where they were, and he wondered what they were supposed to do. The chilly floor made him cold, and he began to miss his warm bed. After a few minutes, small things started to spook him: the occasional creak of packet panels shifting and settling; the drone of a fan motor kicking on.

What if Chip was stuck out there? What if his dad found them both in the morning? What if his parents knew he had snuck out tonight and were waiting for him in the living room? But now the steel gates were opening. A packet was coming in. Seconds later, his dog was in his arms, licking him on the face.

They ran most of the way home through the darkened streets and crept into the quiet house. After his exhausting day, all Martin wanted was to get into bed. But once there, his dreams were torture. In his sleep, he thought he could hear banging on the thick steel plates of the dome. Bug stood outside in a cloud of blowing sand, screaming to be let in.

CHAPTER FIVE

The next day was Rest Day, traditionally devoted to an afternoon nap and the best meal of the week. When Martin smelled brownies, he thought about Bug's cooker never making desserts and went into the kitchen to eat a piece in his memory.

Mom was sitting on the living room floor with her eyes closed, breathing in and out slowly in time to quiet music. On the television, three women in color-coordinated workout clothes were sitting there and breathing too.

"Where's Dad?" Martin wanted to know. "Isn't his fishing show on now?"

"Your father had to go in to work," Mom said, opening her eyes and adjusting her sweatband. "Thank goodness! That fishing show is so boring." She closed her eyes and went back to breathing.

"Work on a Rest Day? What's up?"

"The bots called. Some emergency," Mom said between breaths.

Martin wandered back to his room. All the flavor had gone out of his brownie.

A couple of hours later, Dad returned. "Great news, Tris!" he said, kissing Mom. "The best possible news."

"What is it?" she asked. But Martin was on hand, dishing out another brownie, so Dad smiled and shook his head.

"Let's just say we found something that's been lost," he said, reaching into the refrigerator for a beer.

Good news? What kind of good news? Martin abandoned his plans for the rest of the day and devoted the afternoon to some serious espionage. Cassie begged him to come to the park with her, but he sent Chip in his place. Matt and David joyfully reported that they had installed blender demons in all the ImCity kitchens, but he didn't go admire the carnage. Instead, he loitered in the hallway just out of sight of his parents, memorizing the pattern of picture-hanging holes in the wallpaper. He had long ago memorized the pattern of the wallpaper itself.

During *This Week in Sports History*, his persistence paid off. Dad couldn't contain himself any longer.

"There he was, Tris!" he said. "Right there in the loading bay. Security was holding him, and a darn good thing, too. He was raving like a broken bot."

"You're talking about . . . ," Mom said in a low voice, and Martin heard Dad's recliner creak.

"That's right! And right before this . . . before everything gets started! I was afraid they were going to find us off in our body count. Who knows what would have happened? But no worries now. Perfect timing!"

"Where had he been?" Mom asked quietly.

"Oh, who cares? He looks like hell, out of his gourd, too, hair all over like I don't know what. Social took him down to quarantine and gassed him for me, so there'll be no trouble tomorrow. Pickup's at nine thirty."

"Poor JoAnne," sighed Mom. "Did you tell her and Ben?"

"Of course not! They might file an appeal, and I'm not risking that right now. Besides, it's better that they don't know. You should see his face, Tris. He does look bad."

So they got Bug, Martin thought. How did he get back inside? It was weird that he wasn't dead, but maybe the poison air outside had made him go crazy. Well, crazier, anyway.

The front door opened, and Cassie caught him crouching in the hallway. She giggled, but he motioned for silence, and she and Chip followed him into his room. "Your dog made me come home," she said. "He was a wreck without you." Chip greeted him the way a starving man greets a pepperoni pizza.

What if people found out his dog had led Bug outside? But maybe Bug was too crazy to tell on him.

"Are you listening to me?" Cassie's little face was stern. "You shouldn't lurk around in the hall. You looked like some kind of criminal."

"I just like to know things," Martin said vaguely. And what about the keypad on the elevator door? Did it store the times and dates of log-ins? He should have thought of that.

"What good does it do you to know things?" Cassie said. "You never do anything about it, and you never tell what you find out. We Exponents share our knowledge with the community to help make it a better place."

And then there were the freight bots, Martin thought. How had they called his father? Could they tell their packet chief about Chip? "No one in the community wants to know what you Xs know," he said. "You guys just learn school-type stuff."

"Okay, what have you learned today with your spying?"

"None of your business."

"There, you see? No good to anybody."

But Martin wasn't listening. Nine thirty, he thought. That must be a packet's arrival time. He had to find a way to be there.

> > > >

Next morning, Cassie protested when Martin brought Chip along on the walk to school. "Mom wouldn't like this," she said, stopping to pull a curl out from under her backpack strap. "Mom says toys need to stay at home."

"Yeah, but she won't find out," he said. "She's gone to her stained-glass lesson. And Chip knows his way around, don't you, boy? He can let himself in before she gets back."

At the schoolyard, Chip was aloof but not impolite to the children who crowded around to stroke his rough coat. When the bell rang, Martin waited for the playground to clear and then held a conference with him.

"Look, computer chip," he whispered into the velvety pricked ears, "we have to meet a packet car at nine thirty so I can see what they're doing with Bug. That means you've got to get me out of class. Interrupt school until the teacher sends me out. Don't do anything nontoy, like bite anybody or talk bot, because everyone will be watching. And don't believe me if I tell you not to come back. I'll have to say that. Just keep showing up till the teacher makes me leave."

Those intelligent eyes drank him in, and Chip wagged, but Martin wanted to be sure he understood.

"I'll tell you to go away," he said. "I'll even tell you to go home, but I mean for you to come back, no matter what I say. But not right away. Give it five or ten minutes."

Martin came through the doorway of his classroom a fraction of a second before the tardy bell rang. The mere sight of the place was enough to sap his energy and ruin his mood. Maybe it was the vomit green color of the walls, or maybe it was all those identical desks in rows. No amount of interesting decoration ever made up for the rigid lines of desks.

Martin's teacher seemed to agree. Mr. Ramsey seldom spoke above a halfhearted monotone. Only a few years out of school himself, he was stuck in a classroom while his less gifted peers sat at home drawing factory salaries. "Last as usual, Martin," he remarked with a touch of envy.

"Yes, sir," Martin said. He stuffed his backpack under his chair and plugged his handheld into the desk. The screen jumped a bit as it synchronized itself with the school computer.

"Class, bring up the first exercise," Mr. Ramsey said. Sighing quietly, they did so. "Now, enter these answers as I give them to you: For number one, a. For number two, c. For number three, . . ."

Martin blinked at his handheld in surprise, then glanced sideways to discover his classmates doing the same thing. Why was Mr. Ramsey giving them the answers? There was no time to ask or even wonder. They came so quickly that he had to scramble to catch up.

"For number seventeen, e," continued the teacher. "Martin, is that your dog?"

Martin looked up, startled, and Chip licked him on the nose, tail thumping against a neighboring desk. "Oh! Yes, sir, he is," Martin replied, trying to fend him off.

"And why is he in class?"

"Well, sir, he likes to be with me. I let him come along on the walk to school, so maybe he decided to stay here."

"This is not the time for foolishness," said Mr. Ramsey severely. "Principal Thomasson is visiting our class this morning, and she'll be here any minute. Get that toy out of here."

Martin hustled his dog to the classroom door. "Okay, the plan's off," he whispered. "If the principal sees you here, I'll get in huge trouble. You go home and wait for me. Understand?"

Chip wagged. *I understand perfectly*, his dark eyes seemed to say.

"No, you don't get it!" hissed Martin. "She keeps the permanent records! She can change what jobs we get. I don't want her mad at me. Go home!" Chip trotted off down the hall.

"For number twenty-nine, b. For number thirty, d. Do not press submit. Put your hands in your laps."

There was a knock at the door. The little gray-eyed woman who was their principal entered the room, and every student sat up straighter. Martin saw Mr. Ramsey straighten up too. The principal was that kind of person. Mr. Ramsey led them in a chorus of "Good morning, Principal Thomasson." She nodded gravely in return.

"We residents of Suburb HM1 are very lucky people," she declared. "Matt Johnson, can you tell me why?"

"Because we won?" croaked Matt. He looked wretched. Martin could sympathize. It was a very bad sign when the principal remembered a student's name. Unfortunately, Martin's name was one she had learned long ago.

"That's right," she said. "Our grandparents competed for the right to live here in comfort. The nation faced sickness, poverty, certain death. You in the front row, how many survived?"

A brown-haired girl dimpled, happy to be anonymous. "No one knows the exact number, but—"

"*Don't* embellish!" Principal Thomasson thundered, and the girl's dimples collapsed.

The principal's gray eyes raked across the classroom. "Martin Glass!" she barked, and he jumped and quivered. "How many survived?"

"A few," he said, and her gimlet gaze softened ever so slightly.

"That's right," she confirmed. "A few. Who did more than just survive. We thrive. We have everything we could possibly want. Happiness is not just our right. It is our duty."

The students gazed at her in reverent dread, and she nodded with satisfaction.

"Next week, we will do a few things differently to make our gratitude and happiness more apparent. But first, will someone please tell me: What is that thing?"

Chip was standing on his hind legs at one of the open windows. His head showed above the window frame, and his tan paws were hooked over the sill. Mr. Ramsey snapped around to glare at Martin, and Martin felt his face grow hot.

"Whose toy is that?" demanded Mr. Ramsey.

"Mine, sir," Martin said. His face was flaming now. "I'll get rid of him, don't you worry."

He held a consultation with Chip at the window. "I mean it this time!" he whispered. "She better not see you again!" His dog slunk away, wagging uncertainly.

The principal waited for the disturbance to die down. Then she continued her speech. "Starting next Workday One, and for the whole of next week, we will make our gratitude a little more clear in our orderly behavior. An adult from your street will collect you house by house and walk you to school in the morning. Wait inside your houses until called for. That same adult will collect you on the playground and walk you home. You will not visit friends or play outside in uncontrolled groups. Instead, you will stay indoors. Suitable sports, organized by Mr. Ellis and Mr. Ramsey, will take place in the park during the evenings. They will let you know if you are on one of the teams."

A whole week as bad as school! Martin didn't dare groan at this unwelcome news. David gave him a little kick, as if to say, *What did we do to deserve this?* Martin gave no answering sign.

"Most importantly, we will spend our time outside of school each day watching our television sets. Through judicious programming and advertising, our government notifies us of wholesome products, and we spend our money on them to keep our country strong. During recess, we will sing rhymes from the latest commercials, and I expect you to know the— Good gracious!"

The class turned to see a most unusual Chihuahua sneaking in through the open window. Pea green, to blend in with the classroom's color scheme, the little dog made its way up the side of the wall, its small paws making plopping sounds. It crossed the ceiling, navigating the spaces between the light fixtures. When it reached the spot above Martin's desk, it stopped. There it stayed, hanging upside down from its four paws, its large ears dangling like streamers.

The principal stared at it in astonishment. "Martin Glass, can you explain this?"

Martin's face smoldered with embarrassment. He was sure the neck of his T-shirt was about to catch fire. "Ma'am, I told him that you didn't want to see him anymore." His voice squeaked, and some students snickered. "Anyway, I—I think he's trying really hard not to be seen."

"He is not succeeding," she noted grimly. "We can all see him without difficulty."

"Yes, you're right, I know. I—I think I better take him home. Look, I'm really sorry about all this," he added, and the snickers and giggles got louder.

The small dog disengaged itself from the ceiling and reformed itself as it dropped through the air so that it could land right side up. Once on the ground, it expanded quickly and quietly into a German shepherd again, like a fountain bubbling outward from its base. In seconds, Chip was back, licking Martin's hand. The entire class was breathless at the sight.

"Man!" David said. "My cat never does cool stuff like that!"

"David, you will report to afternoon detention," Principal Thomasson snapped. Martin hurried from the room before she could send him there too.

He ran down the hallway, out the front doors, and across the playground as fast as he could. By the time he arrived at the loading bay elevator, he was completely out of breath. At least now his hands had a reason to be shaking.

"Okay," he said, collapsing against the metal door next to his dog. "Okay, we need to work on that when-you-shouldn't-listen-to-me thing." He paused for breath, and Chip gave him a repentant lick. "Okay. But you did get us out of there, and we have time to find a good place to hide. Remember, Dad better not see us. He'd be furious if he knew I was skipping class."

Martin typed in Dad's password to call the elevator, and they rode it down to the bottom. But they didn't exit through the freight door. Instead, they left the elevator by the small door in the back and worked their way through a maze of hallways and storage rooms. When they reached a wide corridor that opened directly onto the loading bay, Martin found them a hiding place behind a pile of pallets. From there, they could see the steel gates and the main line that the incoming packet would take.

Martin knelt on the concrete floor and peeked through the crack between the pallets and the wall to watch the freight bots rolling back and forth at their work. Chip lay beside Martin with his muzzle on his paws, not looking at anything in particular. Time dragged, but Martin reflected that it could be worse. He could be in class right now.

"I wonder where Bug's going," he whispered to Chip. "I wish there was some way to find out."

At nine thirty, the steel gates swung open, and a modest-size packet pulled in. It actually had windows, clear glass windows just like a house. Martin had never seen windows on a packet before.

A door at the end of the packet slid open, and a trim blond woman emerged. She wore a white lab coat, a pink shirt, and black slacks. In one hand she held a small leather bag. Dad walked over to her, and Martin realized how short she was: the top of her head barely cleared Dad's chin. They talked together for a minute or two, but they were too far away for Martin to hear what they said. Then Dad went back to his console, and the woman walked straight toward the corridor that hid Martin and his dog.

In a panic, Martin looked around for more cover. There was none to be had. The stack of pallets hid them from the front, but not from the side. Crouching against the wall, he pulled up his knees to make himself as small as he could and motioned for

Chip to lie still. The woman in the lab coat passed by not five feet from them, her face set in a look of pleasant expectation.

For some inexplicable reason of his own, Chip jumped to his feet to greet her. Martin grabbed him before he could intercept her, and the woman walked off, unheeding. The fluorescent lights sent bright glimmers across her collar-length hair as she made her way to a turn in the corridor.

Martin watched her till she was out of sight, then turned to his dog. "What are you, crazy?" he hissed. Ears back, Chip thumped his tail halfheartedly, and Martin hyperventilated for a few seconds. "Oh no! She's bound to come back this way! We'd better find another— No, too late!"

The gentle murmur of the woman's voice was coming toward them. There was nothing to keep her from seeing them as she made her way back to the loading bay. Martin could only curl up as close as he could to the pallets and hope that she wouldn't glance over.

And then he saw Bug.

The bearded man was staggering, sliding his feet along the floor so that his whole body swayed from side to side. Dark blood crusted on his arms and in his hair. The little woman led him slowly down the hallway, watching him closely and talking soothingly to him. "You're going to like the trip," she said. "I'll let you sit by the window. You'll see, we're going to have fun."

It was impossible to say whether Bug was taking any of this in. He was barely able to stay on his feet. At one point, he jerked his head to avoid falling, and Martin caught a glimpse of his face. His mouth hung open, and a bit of froth had strayed into his beard. His red-rimmed eyes seemed devoid of life.

None of this disturbed the woman. She leaned close to her shabby companion. "We're going to a wonderful place. I know you'll be glad when you see it." Her small hand was locked around Bug's grimy wrist like a living handcuff.

To Martin's boundless horror, Chip jumped out in front of her. But he didn't growl. From deep within him came the vibrating tone of bot speech.

The woman stopped at once and glanced their way.

What she might have said to them was lost in confusion because at that moment, Bug saw them too. A long bellow, inarticulate and dreadful, emerged from his cracked lips. Again and again, he called out, shouting and then screaming, a frantic cry for help.

The blond-haired woman didn't seem to mind. Smiling blandly, she resumed her platitudes. Then, as Bug thrashed, she simply picked him up and hoisted him over her shoulder. "Such a nice place," Martin heard her say as she walked off. "I'm sure you'll like it when you get there."

The next half hour passed by in a blur. Martin came to himself again at his own front door. Chip stood on the step, and Martin had a vague idea that he had followed the dog home. He could taste acid in his mouth. Had he been throwing up?

His mother's shocked expression brought his wits back, and he stood in the doorway for several seconds, trying to think of something to say.

"Sick . . . sent home," he managed to mutter, but Mom had already come to this conclusion herself. She marched him straight to bed, and he obeyed without protest. This reaction worried her even more.

"You don't have a temperature," she said. "Still, you're very warm. Try to tell me what hurts."

What hurt? Everything. His memory. His idea of safety. His ears, still echoing with Bug's shrieks. "My stomach," he groaned, hugging it. That was something every kid could rely on.

Mom looked relieved. "I thought so," she said, tucking the blanket under his chin. "Maybe it was the milk. I thought it smelled odd. Oh dear, I hope your father's not ill! He was expecting a very important packet." Under the covers, Martin curled up like a shrimp. He didn't want to think about that very important packet anymore.

After Mom left, he lay without moving, trying as hard as he could not to remember. A heavy body jumped onto the bed and lay down at his back, and he was glad to have Chip close by. Hours passed as he slipped in and out of sleep. Eventually, he began to feel better. He reached over to flip on his plasma lamp and watched the green and purple paisley shapes circle the room. Feeling restless, he felt around on the floor by his bed and found a game cartridge. Alien spaceships melted like shaved ice before his devastating onslaught, and he began to perk up.

He turned on the bedside light. The plasma shapes, now nothing more than pale hints of color, continued to slide across the walls. Chip lifted his head and put his ears back in a friendly way, and Martin rubbed the thick, doubled fur of his ruff.

"You know, Chip, Bug was kinda out of control," he said. Chip laid his head down on Martin's stomach and watched him with one dark eye. "Anyway, that lady seemed nice. Not like policemen in the movies. And even if criminals die on the game shows, that doesn't mean Bug's going there. He didn't do anything wrong. He's probably being taken to a special first-aid station, maybe getting cured. He needed that. He looked really bad. She said he'd like it when he got there."

This made him think of something else, and he sat up quickly, dislodging Chip, who scrambled about a bit before righting himself and lifting his head again.

"And what do you think you were doing, jumping out to meet her when we were hiding? You were a bad dog!" At the ultimate reproach, Chip pawed him again and uttered a short bark of protest. "Hey, no back talk! Just for that, get off the bed."

Chip jumped to the floor, ears askew. Once there, he crouched with his head down and whined.

"I guess you think you know better than me, huh? Shame on you! I told you not to speak bot around people."

Quite suddenly, the cringing shepherd ceased to be a dog. Its form flowed from horizontal to vertical. A three-foot-high copy of the trim blond woman stood beside Martin's bed now, looking cheerful and holding out her leather bag.

"Whoa!" Martin gasped, flinging himself back on his pillow and away from the apparition. The miniature woman smiled. She took a step toward him, and he panicked completely. "Mom!" he yelled. *"Mom!"*

Running footsteps thumped down the hall, and his door crashed open. "What's the matter?" his mother cried. For answer, Martin pointed at the little phantom, but the blond woman had disappeared. In her place was Chip, wagging contritely.

"Oh! Hey, boy," said Mom. She bent to pat Chip on the head. "Martin, you just had a bad dream."

Martin gawked at the dog for a second or two. "Yeah," he murmured faintly. "It was bad."

Mom sat down on the bed. "Is your stomachache better?" she asked, feeling his forehead. "Are you ready for food yet? Maybe? Yes? Okay, I'll go get you something."

She went away and left him alone with his pet. Chip seemed to realize that this was an awkward moment. He flopped onto his back, exposing his pale belly and asking for a tummy rub. Martin declined to give him one.

"Man, that was creepy!" he said, shuddering. "Don't scare me like that! So you mean she was a bot, like you. That makes sense, you know—because that's how she could pick him up. Poor Bug!"

Chip began to whine unhappily, and Martin gave in.

"Come here," he said, and he scratched the shepherd behind the ears. "I'll say this for you bots. At least you're nice. I mean, you really care about what you're doing. Like that woman: I would have gotten mad at Bug for shouting and stuff, but she was really sweet. Well, *it* was sweet, anyway. Or at least it acted sweet. Yuck!" He shuddered again.

Cassie came home while he was eating some crackers and entertained him with the news: Principal Thomasson had come to the Wonder Babies' classes and had scolded them for failing to participate with the other students.

"Jimmy said that all the other students do is beat us up," Cassie told him. "And she said that's what we deserve for failing in our civil duty. Or was it civic duty? Martin, which one's right?" He shrugged, and she went on. "Anyway, she said we don't have any student rights as long as we refuse to follow the approved curriculum. But Jimmy says the school's curriculum isn't education at all. He says it's designed to deaden intellectual curiosity."

"He's got that right," Martin sighed.

They heard the bang of the garage door and Dad humming as he walked in. "Cassie, set the table!" Mom called.

Martin wandered out to the living room in time to see his father sink into the big green recliner and tip back the seat. "How's the boy, then?" Dad asked affably, giving Chip a generous scratch behind the ears. "And how's my other boy? I hear you've been sick all day."

"I'm okay," Martin said. "Hey, Dad, how did today go? Mom said you had an important packet."

"Couldn't have gone smoother," Dad said, stretching out in his chair. "Hand me that pillow, would you?" He picked up the remote. "Now, what'll we watch? A little fishing?"

"No, I better go help with dinner," Martin said. He felt better. His father looked perfectly normal, and that meant Bug was wrong. Nobody had sent him off to die. Martin imagined Bug in a first-aid room, having his bloody arms bandaged, maybe even getting a shave.

Cheered, he turned to leave and almost fell over his dog. Chip sat like a statue, staring fixedly at a point on the living room wall. At first, Martin thought he might be hypnotized by the blue- and green-toned spirals of Mom's plate-painting projects. Then Martin discovered a sequinlike object stuck to the wall beside them.

"Hey!" he yelped, pointing.

Dad brought the recliner forward with a snap.

"Stop that!" He grabbed Martin by the shoulder and hustled him over to the couch. "You heard what I said in the loading bay. You are *not* to take notice of those!"

"But, Dad, in our house!"

"Of course, in our house—in all the houses, or will be by Rest Day, when the transmitter gets in. Now, I'll tell you the one thing we don't need, and that's you and a bunch of your idiot friends fooling around with these things. From now on, you know nothing about them. Nothing about them! Do you understand?"

Martin nodded.

"Good! Now don't mention them again. To anybody! You know why."

Martin glanced toward the tiny device, thinking of the squirmy oval thing that had crawled right through his living room and deposited it there to do its work.

"You're right, Dad," he said in a husky voice. "The walls really do have ears."

CHAPTER SIX

Martin went over to David's house after school the next day to help with the zombification of the ImCity cartridge. He sat on David's bedroom floor, tinkering with different settings, while his creations blasted the tidy little neighborhoods into rubble. Flesh-eating spirits haunted the burned-out floor plans and refused to answer the door.

David was watching the game screens over Martin's shoulder. The scent of his butter-rum bubble gum kept wafting into Martin's face.

"Hoo boy!" he cried. "Did you see the look on that postman's face when the goblins ripped off his mailbag?"

"He didn't really look different," said Martin. "I think he's only designed to look one way."

"Wouldn't it be great if we could do this for real? We'd have monsters roaming the streets!"

Martin remembered the energetic woman in the lab coat. "Nah, real life's weird enough for me."

The aroma of butter rum dissipated. A few seconds later, Chip leapt to his feet and barked. Martin turned to find David stepping cautiously toward the dog. Chip's hackles were up, and he was backing away.

"You better not!" Martin jumped up and pried the purple chip from David's hand. "You know what I said about resetting him!"

"Yeah, yeah, you'll pound me," David said carelessly. "But,

listen, this'll be great. We'll take Cinder's circuit board and put them in your dog's gel to make a cat as big as a dog."

Martin had a fleeting vision of a German shepherd–size house cat. Mom would have a fit!

"No way," he said. "My dog's sensitive about resets."

"So what? Okay, if you don't like that idea, then let me hook the handheld to his board to see how he walks on walls. I don't know what I did wrong with Cinder."

Martin gave David's gray cat a sympathetic rub behind the ears. Cinder woke up and purred. She was curled up in a neat circle on the wall by David's desk next to a poster of the Bruised Bananas.

"She walks on walls, all right," Martin said.

David tossed a foam dart at his pet. "Yeah, but now she won't come near the floor."

"Well, you're not gonna mess up my dog like that. Come on, Chip, let's go."

"Hey, wait! What about the game?" David asked, following him down the hall. "You know we won't get a chance to work on it next week, thanks to those loser freaks."

"Says who?" Martin wanted to know, pausing on David's doorstep.

"Says Principal Thomasson," David answered. "She says we gotta be walked to school like a marching band, and no playing outside."

"No, who says that's because of the Exponents?"

"Says everybody," David said. "To keep us from picking on them, because Jimmy complained. Stupid brats! Not your sister, though," he added without much conviction.

"You're a moron," snapped Martin. "This marching-to-school thing isn't about my sister or any of the other Xs." In a flash, he remembered the sequins lining the suburb's walls. Of course! It was about the inspection.

As he stepped into the street, he glanced up at the steel dome overhead. On one side, the skylights glowed brightly, like gigantic light fixtures. On the other side, they were dark and dull, as if it were already night. While Martin watched, the brilliant skylights rapidly dimmed and a gray pall fell over the suburb.

Bug had been outside and had come back a drooling madman. What had he seen out there? Had he found a world so different from theirs that he couldn't stand the sight of it?

"You've got this really stupid look on your face," David said.

"David! Hey, David, guess what!"

Matt came charging around the corner, wildly excited. Then he saw Martin and stopped.

"Well, what, doofus?" David asked.

"Nothing," Matt answered. "So, taking off, huh?" he said to Martin. His face wore the same expression Dad's did whenever something important happened at work.

"You better go ahead and tell me," Martin said. "I'm not leaving till you do."

Matt shrugged. "Okay, but don't get mad at me. So I was hanging around the basketball hoops, watching the big guys play, and they started griping about how they wouldn't be able to finish their tournament next week, you know, because of the Wonder Babies."

"*Not* because of the Wonder Babies," Martin said.

Matt shrugged again.

"So anyway, they said they oughta teach the little freaks a lesson for running to the principal, so that's what they're doing right now. They knocked teeth out of this one first grader down by the swings. David, you gotta come watch!"

"Oh no! Cassie!" cried Martin. "David, did she say she was going home? Did she go to Julie's?"

"How should I know?" David said. Martin took off running.

Cassie wasn't at Julie's house. Julie thought she might be at Jessica's. But what if Cassie had gone to the park instead? Martin didn't know what to do.

"Chip, run home and see if Cassie's there," he said. "If she is, I want you to keep her there. If she isn't, check the park. Find her and don't let anybody mess with her. Do whatever you have to."

Chip sped off down the street like a large furry bullet.

Martin was gasping for air by the time he reached Jessica's house. Cassie wasn't there, but another little blond girl was, and she was crying. Jessica told him the girl was afraid to go home.

"Brandon came by and told us they knocked out Arthur's teeth," Jessica said. "Abigail lives by the park. They're bound to catch her on the way home."

"But it's almost dinnertime," sobbed the little girl. "I said I'd be home before dinner."

"You live near us," Martin said. "I can get you home."

Oh, that's great, you moron, his brain remarked. Cassie needs help, and you're taking on charity cases!

The little girl laced her sneakers, and they set off. She trotted along bravely, but her legs were so short that Martin thought they were barely moving. "Fighting is wrong, isn't it?" she wanted to know. He ignored the question at first. But when he glanced down, her big blue eyes were riveted on his, and she looked eerily like Cassie.

"I guess it is," he said.

"If it's wrong, then why don't the adults ever try to stop it?"

This is all I need, he thought. On top of everything else, I'm stuck with an Exponent trying to learn something meaningful from the threat of getting beat up. "I dunno," he muttered. "It's just one of those things people turn their back on." That phrase upset him, and he hurried to replace it. "Mr. LaRue says it's good for us kids; it teaches us to get along."

She looked puzzled. "How can we draw lessons of social concord from acts of capricious violence?"

"I dunno. Listen, Abby—"

"It's Abigail."

Martin counted to ten.

"Listen, Abigail, we've gotta get somewhere, so you need to shut up, okay?" And he sped up his walk so that she would have to run.

They walked by house after house of soft pink brick, surroundings so familiar that he felt more than saw the houses pass by: picture window, front door, garage, and the slant of a driveway. They turned a corner and walked down the short side of a block. The houses changed to slate blue, but the pattern was the same: picture window, front door, garage, and the slant of a driveway. Martin could have found his way home blindfolded.

The street curved, and a scene of capricious violence came into view. Two big boys stood over a smaller one, pummeling him with their fists.

"It's Jimmy!" Abigail cried.

Jimmy crouched on the curb, holding his stomach. "I don't see—what you're hoping—to gain by this," he gasped. "I've already said—I surrender."

"We don't care what you say," said one of the boys, reaching down to smack him on the ear. Martin knew the boy but didn't like him. He had a big nose, and he snored whenever he fell asleep in class.

Patches sat up on Jimmy's shoulder and bared his buckteeth in a long hiss, lashing his hairless tail from side to side. "Hey, look at the freak's toy!" shouted the other boy. He seized the thick tail, whirled the rat around in an arc, and launched him into space.

"Patches!" Jimmy shrieked.

The rat hit the sidewalk and rolled end over end, squealing the whole time. The second he managed to right himself, he was off in a black-and-white streak. In an instant, he vanished down a drain.

"Patches!" Jimmy cried again. Then he burst into loud tears.

Martin felt the blood sing in his ears and lurched forward, swinging his fists. Then everything seemed to happen in a fast blur, like those fights in cartoons. "You messed with his *rat*!" he heard himself shouting. "Don't *mess* with a little kid's *rat*!" He felt the jolt of his fists landing again and again.

The scene came back into focus, and he saw the two boys gaping at him as if he were a monster out of a horror movie. A bright stream of blood flowed from the snorer's big nose, and he looked like he was going to faint. Martin raised his fists again, and the two boys took off down the street. He sucked on a split knuckle and watched them go.

Jimmy had crept to the drain and was calling his pet in a husky whisper.

"Doesn't he have to obey you?" Martin asked.

"No, he doesn't," Jimmy said. He tried to sound matter-of-fact, but his voice trembled and his face twitched with pain and misery. "He doesn't. I told you, he's *real*. I don't think he's coming back."

Martin helped the leader of the Exponents limp to the curb. He talks like an adult, but he's not, Martin thought. He's still just a little kid. The blond girl stood on the sidewalk, crying so hard that she couldn't see. That's all they are, thought Martin, herding them both down the street. They're just a bunch of little kids.

He walked Jimmy to his front door and listened while Jimmy's mother chewed the boy out. "I can't believe it!" she cried. "I send you to the store for one item, just one item, and you get yourself in another fight!"

"It wasn't his fault, ma'am," Martin said, but she spread her hands as if to push his words away.

"He has to learn how to get along with people. He has to!"

When Martin arrived at his own house at last, he found Chip in front of Cassie's bedroom door. The dog greeted Martin as enthusiastically as oxygen entering an air lock.

Cassie was sitting on her bed, typing away on her handheld. "Your dog has been pretty strange," she said. "He tried to follow me into the bathroom, and when I told him no, he stood in the hall and howled."

Martin gave Chip a hug. "Good dog!"

Cassie giggled. "If that's what you call it."

Martin sat down on the bed and watched her type for a

minute, thinking about what he had seen. She was so skinny and little. She could get hurt so easily.

"I don't want you playing at your friends' this week," he said. "If you're not in this house, I want you with me." He hoped she would argue with him or, better yet, laugh at him. But the look in her eyes told him that she understood perfectly, and this made him feel even worse.

"It's okay," she said. "I have work to do. Next week, I have to teach the class about isomers and isotopes."

"Hoo boy!" muttered Martin.

"Dr. Church lost on yesterday's show," she said. "They asked him for six commercial uses of calcium carbide, and he knew only four. We Exponents are already missing him."

Martin tried not to think about the old man. He was a criminal, he reminded himself. He deserved it. It's like Mom says: just turn your back.

"Maybe they'll have him on the show again," Cassie said, "since he was so famous."

Martin flopped back on the bed to stare at the ceiling. Chip took this as an invitation to jump up and curl into a big fuzzy ball beside him. "I doubt it, Cass," he said wearily, petting his dog.

"Do you want to hear what I've got ready to teach so far? It's about alpha decay and beta decay."

About as much as I want my teeth drilled, Martin thought. But he remembered Jimmy and stopped just in time.

"Sure, Cass," he said. Then he spent the next half hour perfecting an interested expression.

Dinner was a gloomy affair. Dad was delayed at work so long that Mom decided to serve the meal without him.

"Martin, eat your brandied pepper steak," she said. "I spent all afternoon on it."

"Sorry?" he asked vaguely, struggling to unknot his brain from gamma rays and neutrinos. He hadn't been exposed to so much science in weeks. It had left him feeling mutated.

"All afternoon!" Mom repeated. "If I don't get three red diamonds in a row on the cooker, it doesn't make brandied pepper steak!"

"Three diamonds," he speculated. "Doesn't that come up, like, every eight thousand tries?"

"Odds of one in four thousand," corrected Cassie. "There's two diamonds per reel. You're thinking of three lemons in a row: prime rib."

"Oh, wow! Prime rib." Martin was jolted out of his academic muddle by the memory of succulent beef. "Man, I wish we could have prime rib again."

"Cassie!" Mom scolded. "It isn't right to know all that math." His little sister visibly deflated at the rebuke, and Martin lost his temper.

"Look, I don't see what's wrong with it! So she's smart. They're all smart! What's the problem? Why can't people leave them alone? Beating them up, slinging Jimmy's rat down a drain—"

"No!" said Cassie.

"He asks for it," Mom said grimly. "Walking around here like he thinks he's better than everyone else."

"Yeah, and maybe he's right!" Martin said. "He's smarter, looks better, a whole lot nicer—"

"Martin!"

"So maybe he *is* better, what about that? Maybe he really is!"

The door opened, and Dad came in. He stumbled over the step from the garage as if he were very tired, or very old.

"Walt, you need to tell your son to mind his manners!"

Dad didn't answer her. He stopped at his place at the table and stood leaning on his chair, staring down at his plate. They waited for a few seconds, but he didn't make any move to sit down.

"Are you all right?" Mom asked. "You're acting funny."

Dad glanced up. His eyes looked puzzled and a little hurt. He studied them each in turn, as if wondering how they came to be there. Last of all, his eyes rested on Cassie.

"Daddy?" she whispered.

But Dad didn't seem to have heard. He turned and walked out of the kitchen. They heard his feet shuffle slowly down the hall and the bang of his bedroom door.

"Well! Eat your brandied pepper steak," said their mother.

When the national anthem began playing the next morning, Dad was already out of the house.

"Special business," Mom said. "Very important. He told me to vote for him."

"Is he all right?" Cassie asked in a small voice. Martin knew not to ask. He could tell by the set to his mother's mouth that she didn't understand either.

After school, he wanted to check on Dad, but he had to walk Cassie home. Several of her friends came with them, seeking sanctuary, and he had to drop them off at their houses along the way.

Dad worked late again that night—so late that Mom put his dinner in the refrigerator. Martin had been in bed for some time before he heard his father come home. Immediately, he began to plot his quiet transfer to his listening post by the living room door, but before he could get up, he heard Dad walk by on his way to bed. That put an end to that.

"Special business?" Cassie guessed when her father wasn't in the living room the next morning. Mom just gave a shrug.

That afternoon, Martin was determined to get Cassie safely past the bullies and then sprint back to spend some time in the loading bay. But several more Wonder Babies had black eyes and bruises from encounters the day before, and when school let out, a whole crowd of them tagged along on the walk home. David and Matt stayed away from Martin, dismayed at his obvious weakness of character, but Martin didn't have the heart not to help the children. He shepherded his little charges from street to street, disposing of one after another.

"I wish I had a big brother," a kindergarten boy said solemnly, walking at Martin's side. "But Mama says it's too expensive for the stork to come twice."

Martin hadn't realized before how much his existence sheltered Cassie. Even though Mom got angry with her and Dad lectured her, Martin was there to tickle her, play games with her, and boss her around. Cassie still skipped and giggled in spite of her isotopes. Martin didn't think this small boy had giggled in years.

"I wish you had a big brother too," Martin told him. "Someone's gotta be there to teach you baseball."

"I know about baseball," the little boy said. "The airflow around the stitches creates a turbulence that causes the ball to curve. Baseball is fundamentally about physics."

"That is just so wrong," Martin said sadly, and for the first time in his life, he allowed a child other than Cassie to hold his hand.

And so the workweek went. He found his mornings and evenings embroiled in Wonder Baby difficulties, and Dad simply wasn't around.

Martin woke up on the first day of the weekend determined to find out what was wrong, but Mom announced over the breakfast table that she had other plans. "We're cleaning every square inch of this house," she informed the children, and the stress of the last week showed on her face. Martin knew what he would hear if he argued. It would be useless. The work took them all day.

But today is going to be different, Martin decided when Rest Day dawned. He called Chip and left the house as soon as breakfast was over, before Mom could find anything else for him to do.

When Martin got to the loading bay, his father looked happy to see him. In fact, Dad seemed almost normal. But there was a strange look in his eyes that deepened when Martin tried to tell him about the week he had missed, and Dad kept interrupting his news with short errands. Still mystified, Martin gave up on conversation and sat down on the floor to pet his dog.

Dad was directing the freight bots in cleaning up the loading bay, and Martin had to admit that it was looking nicer than he'd ever seen it. But it hardly seemed like round-the-clock, weeklong work. The freight bots could probably do it on their own. Why was Dad here? he wondered. No packets came on Rest Day. Rest Day . . . The phrase jarred something in his memory.

"Dad, no packets are coming today, right?" he asked.

"Maybe," said his father curtly, and then he walked off.

It's that inspection thing again, thought Martin. That's right. Dad said the transmitter was arriving today.

His father's console began to beep steadily, jerking him out of his thoughts. Dad hurried over to see what had triggered the warning, and Martin jumped up to read the screen over his father's shoulder.

BNBRX ONLINE, read the screen. UNSCHEDULED PACKET APPROACHING YOUR BAY WILL ARRIVE IN ONE HOUR FORTY SEVEN MINUTES

Unscheduled? That must be the transmitter, Martin thought. But Dad was looking puzzled.

HM1 ONLINE, he typed back. WHAT IS PACKETS ORIGIN

BNBRX ONLINE, came the answer. ORIGIN UNKNOWN POINTS VISUAL INDICATES SELF GUIDED TRANSPORT CONFIRMS A HUMAN AT THE CONTROLS

"A human?" Martin asked.

"A human!" Dad exclaimed. "Martin, you'd better go."

The screen blinked for a few seconds and then lit up.

PACKET CHIEF GATHER YOUR SUBURB, it read. MANDATORY ALL FAMILIES ATTEND

HM1 ONLINE, Dad typed. FRED IS THAT YOU

But his message died away before he could finish. The console screen went black.

CHAPTER SEVEN

The news spread as fast as eager children could run from house to house. A stranger was coming to their suburb! By the time the mysterious packet rolled through the steel gates, every single resident was waiting to greet it in the crowded funeral room. They had to shout to hear one another over the din.

"Maybe it's one of those giveaways," suggested David to Matt and Martin. "Maybe it's a taste test, and we'll get to pick a new flavor. Let's pick the one that's really bad and see if it gets its own commercial."

Alarm bells beeped in the loading bay. A long packet rolled through the doors of the octagonal chamber and stopped in their midst. Never in Martin's years of watching his father at work had he seen a packet like this. It was bright, shiny red with big glass windows down the sides, a jolly sight in that dismal room.

The door at the front slid open, and a young man stepped out, the first stranger most of them had ever met. He was every bit as remarkable as his transport, good-looking and tall, with thick chestnut hair and brown eyes. He had an indefinable appeal— star quality, like a television actor—and he smiled easily, as if he were used to the public eye. He was wearing golf pants of bright red and yellow plaid, and his sweater, red with yellow diamonds, continued the flamboyant color scheme. It was too much to say that the two articles of clothing matched, but at least they seemed to get along.

His outrageous outfit might have annoyed the adults present, but it acted on the Wonder Babies like a magnet. It suggested happy things to the little children: toys and the circus, a pledge of thrilling events to come. They wormed their way through the crowd until they stood in a fascinated throng at his feet.

The adults and older children drew back to let the little ones through. They didn't want to be too close to the packet in case the gaudy visitor did something embarrassing, like ask them to sing or pick volunteers for a contest. But Martin moved forward to keep an eye on Cassie. He didn't want her getting too close to a stranger.

"Welcome to suburb HM1," Dad said in a hearty voice. Only Martin could detect the worry underneath it. But the unusual young man wasn't listening. He seemed every bit as interested in the Wonder Babies as they were in him. He had picked up little Laura and was holding her in his arms, having what seemed to be a private conversation.

"You're the youngest of all, aren't you?" he said gently. "You're the baby of the whole suburb."

Laura looked like a picture in her frilly green party dress, and she beamed at the stranger in delight. "Mommy says the stork got tired after bringing me. That old stork's taking a break."

"The stork has definitely had its ups and downs these last two years," the man agreed. He set her on her feet and turned to Martin's father. "I'm sorry, I'm afraid I didn't hear you."

"Welcome to HM1," Dad repeated, less heartily this time. "My name is Walter Glass, and I'm the packet chief here."

But the young man still didn't seem to be listening. Now he was gazing at the ceiling. Martin looked up to see what had caught his attention. A constellation of tiny sequins clung to the panels there, catching the room's golden light and scattering it from dot to dot.

"The transmitter?" the stranger asked softly, gesturing toward the tiny dots.

A spasm of worry crossed Dad's face. "I expect it today."

"And have you received the product recall announcement?" the young man asked. Dad's face sagged like butter under running water. "You have. Excellent! Packet Chief, I expect your full support."

"What's your name?" Laura asked, reaching up to him.

"You can call me Motley," he told her.

"I know why," Cassie said shyly. "It's because you're wearing motley."

"That's right," he said. "And because I'm motley myself, assembled from lots of different parts. Now, you," he continued, bending down to study her, "you're a Model Eleven-A, that's what you are, with a recessive tweak on the fifteenth and nineteenth chromosomes."

Cassie grinned. "Mom wanted blue eyes to remind her of Granny."

This was a bit too cozy for Martin's taste. "Come away, Cass," he ordered, seizing her thin shoulder and pulling her back.

Motley glanced up at the interruption. "You're . . . too old," he mused. And then he looked elsewhere, as if Martin couldn't hold his interest.

Meanwhile, Dad had recovered his composure. "Mr. Motley," he said, "how . . . er . . . what would you like me to do to help?"

"What can you do to help me?" Motley echoed. He stepped

onto the packet car's platform to elevate himself above the assembly.

"I am not here," he shouted, "so that you good people can do something to help me. Instead, I am here to do something for you. I have come to solve your most difficult problem—the problem of your children."

Neighbor turned to neighbor, perplexity on every face. What problem did their children have? Or were their children the problem?

"Aren't we kids supposed to be a problem?" muttered David to Matt.

"Yeah!" Matt whispered back.

"Your youngest children," Motley went on, "are suffering, and so are you. They cannot become what you ask of them, and you cannot give them what they want. So I have been sent here to help you."

An excited ripple of talk ran through the crowd. Martin didn't join in. Of course the Exponents were suffering; no one had to tell him that. But he didn't think he liked this flashy television star for deciding to interfere.

While Motley waited for the noise to die down, Jimmy stepped to the foot of the platform. He looked doubtful too, and his pale face was even more serious than usual. He took a deep breath and automatically reached a hand to his shoulder, but Patches wasn't there. Martin felt a pang of sympathy for him and glanced around to find his dog. Chip laid his ears back, happy to be noticed, and Martin stroked his rough fur.

"Are you really here to help us?" Jimmy asked. "Us children? To solve our problems?"

Motley crouched down on the platform to study him. "You're about eight years old," he remarked. "And carrying the weight of the world on your shoulders. What's your name?"

"I'm Jimmy Ellis."

Motley nodded. "You're the oldest of them. Yes, Jimmy, I am here most particularly to solve your problems. That's why I'm addressing your families." And he straightened up to continue his speech.

"Well, my problem is that I can't find my pet rat," said Jimmy. "Last week, he got lost—hurt maybe." He gulped, and Martin saw him fight back tears. "He hasn't come home, so I think he went back to his old home in the warehouse area. I know there has to be a way to find him, some sort of invention I could make. But I don't know what it is. Do you know anything about rats?"

"As it happens, I know a lot about rats," Motley said. "About rats—and about you children. But I don't have much time. I actually came here to solve a different problem."

Jimmy's face crumpled. "I understand," he said, and Martin saw the weight of the world settle back onto the boy's shoulders.

Motley saw it too.

"You know rats don't live very long," he pointed out kindly.

"Yes, sir," Jimmy replied in a dull voice. "An average life span of two years."

"Besides," Motley said, "your parents have probably tried the same sorts of traps I would try."

Jimmy didn't answer. Of course he won't, thought Martin; he doesn't want to say anything bad about his parents. But he remembered Jimmy's mother yelling at the boy for getting beaten up, and a hot bolt of anger shot through him. "Sir, his parents don't care," he said loudly, and he glowered at Motley's look of surprise. Well, somebody needed to say it, he thought.

"Other grown-ups, then," Motley went on. "Jimmy, surely there's someone here who helps you out with the things you can't do."

Once again, Jimmy didn't answer, but his face gave him away, and the people within earshot became quiet. Martin saw Motley gaze searchingly at the crowd, and he knew what he was seeing. He had seen it himself where Wonder Babies were concerned. No interest. No involvement. No help.

Motley jumped down from the platform. "All right, let's see what we can do in fifteen minutes. Packet Chief, I'll need some supplies: six or eight of the Soundcone wireless speakers, and I think I can work with that home musician's keyboard that comes with the built-in console."

"Naturally," Dad said, trying to suppress his bewildered expression. "I'll talk to Bennett. He runs the store. Does a nice job of it too. In fact . . ." But Motley had already turned away. Dad walked off, muttering.

Again, Martin found himself the object of Motley's thoughtful stare.

"You look like the sort of young man who knows his way around here," he said. "As well as where to find any odds and ends I might need."

"Yes, sir. I spend a lot of time down here. My dad's the packet chief."

"The packet chief's son. Of course you are! Tell me, is there a room in this warehouse area where food gets stored, spilled, maybe left out in the open?"

The produce room! Martin remembered Chip hunting rats by digging through the rotten vegetables. When he glanced down, his dog put his ears back and thumped his tail, as if to say, *I didn't mean to be right.*

"Yes, sir," Martin said. "I think I know just the place."

Motley clapped a hand on Martin's and Jimmy's shoulders and steered them through the crowd. "Excellent! Lead me to it."

The produce room was bright and clean, and the cardboard crates and piles of old fruit peels and melon rinds were gone. The vegetable-cleaning bots stood unmoving at their white porcelain trough.

"Well, normally there's food here," Martin said, dismayed.

But Motley began at once to explore the place. "This is just what I had in mind."

Dad walked in behind them, trailing an interested crowd of Wonder Babies. "You see, no rats here," he said with evident relief.

"They're behind those refrigerators," murmured Motley.

He soon had the whole group hunting through the storage rooms for special parts. "Steel box. Could be a packing case, empty fuel container, old locker." When Martin found a broken refrigerator, Motley was delighted. "Perfect! Packet Chief, I need two freight bots in here."

The bots put the refrigerator on rollers, laid it on its side, and cut a round hole in the door. Motley emerged from a closet with a three-foot-long piece of tin pipe. He pushed the pipe into the hole, angled so that it tilted down to the ground, and then he had the freight bots weld it into place.

"Now we need to blockade the room with something about

this high." Motley held his hand about two feet off the floor. "You wouldn't believe how well rats can jump."

Martin and Dad barricaded the doorway of the produce room with a sheet of metal, pushing it firmly against the doorframe with heavy boxes. The bots rolled the refrigerator over to it. Then they cut a hole at the bottom of the barricade just wide enough for the tin pipe to stick through. Now any small animal that wanted to escape the room had to run into the tin tunnel. From there, it could only end up in the refrigerator.

Motley found a garbage can lid big enough to close off the end of the tunnel. "This isn't a great fit," he said, kneeling to try it over the pipe, "but I think it's close enough. Now, bring me a gas cylinder—the kind used for carbonated beverages."

Bennett showed up with the sets of speakers, and Motley stepped over the barricade to set them in various places around the room. Then he climbed back out and began fiddling with the computer display on the keyboard. When he struck a note, all six speakers in the room played it.

"The audio is ready," he said. "We can start. Once the rats are in this refrigerator, I'll need the freight bots to pull it away from the door and turn it onto its back. And then I'll need a small hole punched in the side of the tin pipe, just big enough to fit this nozzle." He held up the carbon dioxide cylinder. Martin wanted to ask what it was for, but he thought that might make him seem stupid.

"Jimmy, right after that, you'll need to find your rat," Motley continued. "You won't have much time. You can't be squeamish. I'll help you. Does he have any distinguishing marks?"

"He's piebald, white with black patches," Jimmy said. "His

left ear is white, and his right ear is black." Jimmy's face was paler than before. He looked as if he were hoping and trying not to hope at the same time.

Motley concentrated on his little keyboard, holding down one note. "It's not working," Dad said. "I can't hear anything."

"You can't," Motley said. "But they can."

At first, all was silent. Then came a flurry of rustling and protesting squeaks. From beneath the refrigerators poured a tide of small furry bodies, fleeing the noiseless waves of sound.

"Rats!" cried Dad in dismay.

The rats were dammed up for a few seconds at the steel barricade, scrambling this way and that, before they found the metal tunnel and hurried in. Motley watched them flow into his trap. When the last one entered, he clapped the garbage can lid over the end.

"Got them! Now, pull the trap out and set it on its back."

The bots rolled the refrigerator away from the hole in the barricade. As they moved it, Motley had to shift his lid, and several dark forms sprang from the end of the pipe and sped into the crowd of Wonder Babies, causing the children to jump and squeal. But within seconds, the refrigerator rested on its back with the section of pipe sticking straight into the air, and Motley's lid once again covered the end.

"A few got away," he remarked, gazing after the vanished rodents. "But I'm fairly sure they were regular black ones."

A muted but insistent scuffling came from within the refrigerator trap, augmented by louder scrapings inside the pipe. Motley showed one of the freight bots where to punch a hole, shoved the nozzle into it, and began releasing the gas.

"It can leak out at the top," Dad observed.

"Carbon dioxide is heavier than air," Motley said, listening to the sound of the rats inside the refrigerator.

Soon the frantic rustling subsided. When all was quiet, Motley wrenched open the refrigerator door. Inside the insulated box lay the still shapes of dozens of rats. Motley and Jimmy quickly dug through them to get to the ones underneath.

"Here he is!" Jimmy lifted out a limp form. "Patches!" He pulled off his sweater to make a pillow for the rat, and the Wonder Babies crowded around him to stare at the prodigal rodent.

Dad came forward to peer inside the refrigerator. "I get it," he said. "You used the gas to sedate them."

"To knock them out, yes," Motley said, shutting the refrigerator door. "And kill them, if they breathe it long enough. Why don't you pull that water hose over here and fill this up? That will finish them off."

While Dad fetched the hose to exterminate the contents of the refrigerator, Motley came over to check on Jimmy's rat. Patches was starting to stir feebly, cuddled in the safety of his owner's arms.

"You solved my problem!" breathed Jimmy, and his face was streaked with tears. "I was sure I'd never see him again."

Motley put a comforting hand on the boy's shoulder and studied the piebald pet. "Your rat wears motley too," he said softly. "That fits. Let's go now. I have to get back to my packet."

"Don't leave," Jimmy pleaded, walking beside him. "You knew exactly what to do. You know things we want to learn, and no one would mind if you stayed."

Motley smiled down at him. "I have a better idea."

They returned to the big funeral room. As Dad pushed through the crowd, Mr. Bennett tapped him on the shoulder.

"I had Frank run home and see if we were all on television," he said. "The only thing on the sets was a blue screen. Maybe that means we're on. If we're on, we can't see ourselves, right?"

Motley climbed back aboard the platform of his red packet car. With his good looks and flashy clothing, he did look as if he belonged on television.

"Citizens of HM1!" he called. "Here is your problem. These small children, these Wonder Babies, are taxing your patience, and they themselves are unhappy. They cannot meet your expectations of them any more than you can meet theirs. Your school cannot teach them, and more than anything, they want to learn. They have special needs that cannot be met under your steel dome."

A murmur arose at these remarks, but it was thoughtful and receptive. This stranger had indeed put his finger on a problem that they couldn't solve.

"What I propose today will sadden you," he continued, "but I know you will do what's best. Allow me to take them with me to a special school, a place where they can be with their own kind—where at last, they can be the normal ones."

Martin stood still in shock. Take Cassie away? Take *his* little sister?

"Fine with me," he heard someone say behind him.

"Best idea I've heard in years," agreed another.

"I know this will be hard for you all," concluded Motley, "but I need your decision at once so that I can take the children with me today. I'm afraid I can give you only a few minutes to confer. This is a complicated process, and I have other locations to visit."

He stepped down, and the noise swelled to an uproar, as if someone had turned up the volume. Dad waded through the little children around the packet car and climbed up onto the platform, waving his arms. "Quiet! Quiet, please," he called over the mounting din. "All parents of Wonder Babies, follow the steel rails into the loading bay. I'll give you five minutes to assemble. We need to take a vote."

The commotion became even louder after that, with people pushing through the throng and out of the room. Only Martin seemed rooted to the ground, unable to think what to do. Confused thoughts whirled through his mind as he tried to make sense of the situation. Take Cassie? How could the stranger do this to him? Motley had seemed so nice!

Without planning to, he wandered over to the packet car, where the little children had gathered. Chip followed in his wake, and sober-faced Wonder Babies came over to hug the big dog for moral support. Motley sat in the midst of the youngest children, holding baby Laura on his knee. He seemed to be trying to calm them.

"I know you're all sad right now," he said, "but my school is a wonderful place."

A wonderful place. Martin felt as if he had been jolted by an electric current. He couldn't be—no, *it* couldn't be—

"I know you'll be glad when you get there," Motley went on. "You'll see, we'll have fun."

"Oh man, oh man!" breathed Martin, stumbling blindly away. "Oh no! He's one of *them*!"

He shoved and socked and punched his way through groups of protesting people. The paneled wall reeled up in front of him, and he leaned against it, gasping. A worried whimper attracted his attention, and he crouched down to bury his face in Chip's thick fur.

"It all makes sense," he whispered. "He's like the lady who came for Bug! They're not even going to wait for these kids to grow up. They've sent him to get them now. Dad—I've got to talk to Dad!"

The Wonder Baby parents were straggling back out of the loading bay by the time Martin got there. He found his father standing by the inoperative console, trying various keyboard combinations. "Dad, you've got to get rid of this guy!" he said. "He's not like he looks. I mean, he seems nice, but they're *supposed* to seem nice!"

Dad was sweating, and there was a sick look on his face, as if he had just tasted something nasty. "We voted to let the children go to their school," he said. "And that's what's going to happen."

"But, Dad, I think this guy isn't even human. I think he's a bot!"

His father turned, and the strange expression in his eyes scared Martin. "What's wrong with that?" he demanded.

"Well," said Martin, taken aback, "it means that—I don't know—that we can't trust him."

"Why not? What do you know about where he comes from? What do you know about his business? What about the school? Have you been there?"

"No," Martin admitted. "I mean, maybe there's a school. I guess I don't know for sure."

"Stay out of it, then!" Dad snapped, wiping the sweat from his brow, and he went back to work on the console.

I don't believe this, thought Martin, more confused than ever. *I better talk to Mom.*

He found her near the packet car, hugging his little sister. "Well, Cassandra," she was saying.

Cassie's face shone with excitement, even though tears were in her eyes. "If he brought the packet here once, he can do it again," she said. "Maybe for my birthday."

Mom didn't reply. She just stroked Cassie's golden curls, unwinding the soft corkscrews between her fingers. "Better get in line," she said quietly, and Cassie darted off.

"Mom," ventured Martin. "Mom, this isn't right. She shouldn't go."

His mother was watching Cassie join Jessica and Abigail next to the packet car. Cassie caught hold of her friends' hands, and the little girls began jumping up and down.

"You think we should keep her here all alone while the rest of them leave?" asked Mom. "Think how terrible that would be for her. Think how much she'd be hated. Your Dad's right. Cassie needs a school like this where she can be herself."

"But—"

"But what?" she murmured, still looking at his sister.

Martin couldn't explain it. Dad was right. He didn't know, not for sure.

He found himself among the little children again, feeling dazed and numb. Thin arms wrapped around him. Cassie was hugging him tightly.

"Isn't it funny?" she gushed. "You must think we're idiots.

We're so excited over a school, and you just hate school!"

"Yeah," he muttered. "It's pretty weird."

She gave Chip a hug, but the shepherd didn't respond. Instead, Martin's dog was watching him closely, as if there were something he should tell him to do. "Listen, Cass," he said. "About this school. I think—" Yes, he thought, but what did he really know? Then she was smiling at him again, and he lost his nerve.

"I have to get back in line," she said. "We're almost ready. Motley wants us to board by age groups."

"About the school," Martin tried again, walking her over to her class. "Look, I just want to say, if you don't like it, if it's"—he groped for words—"I mean, maybe it's no good. Just remember, I won't leave you there. Not if it's, you know, if you don't like it. I'll come and—and—" But words failed him. He didn't know what he would do.

Cassie looked up at him with her big blue eyes. "I know you will," she said.

"So I'll see you," he said, getting angry. "No matter what! I'll see you later, Cass. I mean it!"

She hugged him again. "See you, Martin," she whispered.

The littlest children were already boarding the packet, lifted up over the steps by the mysterious man in bright plaid. One by one, they were disappearing into the packet car, just like the rats scuttling into his refrigerator. Laura stood on the platform, graciously waving to her sobbing mother, looking like the world's smallest beauty pageant queen.

"I count seven three-year-olds boarded," said Jimmy to Motley, peering at the screen on his handheld. Patches was back on his shoulder now where he belonged.

"I've checked off everyone below four," Motley said, reading his own handheld. "Time to count the four-year-olds and send them inside."

Martin couldn't stand it any longer. "Look, don't think I don't know about this," he accused, barging up to the stranger. "And I'm not letting you get away with it, either."

Motley glanced at him and then quickly gave Jimmy his handheld. "Keep loading them. Use my list." Then he took a step aside. "Now, what is this about?"

"You know," Martin declared. "I'm not letting you haul away my little sister. I know you're one of those lab-coated creeps!"

This shot hit home: dismay flickered across Motley's face. "How do you know about that?" he asked quietly.

"Never mind how," Martin said. "I know a lot. I know about the game shows, too."

Now the man looked stunned. "Exactly what do you know?" he asked, seizing Martin's arm. Chip bristled, curling his black lips away from sharp teeth. "And where did you get your hands on a modified bot?" demanded Motley, even more amazed.

The effect of this comment on Chip was instantaneous. One second, the bot dog was on his feet, growling ferociously. The next second, he was sitting by Martin's side. The change happened faster than a dog could move. To switch moods, he actually transformed.

By then, Motley had recovered his amiable charm. "I know about you, too," he said. "That's how I knew you were the one I needed to help me with my rattrap. You're a Dish Fourteen. No wonder you don't trust me. You're suspicious of anything new. If someone buys your socks in the wrong color, you won't speak to them for two days."

Martin gaped at him. "How do you know that?" he asked. "Did you talk to my mom?"

"No," Motley said. "You didn't have a mother. No offense; I didn't, either. But I'd say that any woman who has put up with a Fourteen for—let's see—thirteen years now has definitely earned the title of 'Mom' the hard way. Your teachers stop her on the street to complain about you. Your grades are terrible. But you always know the things that are really worth knowing."

"Wow!" Martin said. "That's right!" He was jostled by the six-year-olds boarding the car, but he didn't even notice.

"And you're a fantastic big brother," Motley added after a slight hesitation. "You're very protective. Your goal is to be the meanest person in your little sister's world. If anything worse comes along, you'll fight it to the death."

"Right again!" said Martin in amazement. "How did you know?"

Motley laughed. "Let's just say that I have some personal experience. I know a Fourteen well. She's going to be very pleased when I tell her about you."

"Who is she? Is she good in school?"

"She was frightful!" said Motley cheerfully. "Mainly because she was never there. She was always cutting class because she thought school was stupid. She could have done well if she'd wanted to, and so could you. You're very smart, you know."

Martin felt a grin zigzag across his face. "You think so?"

"Absolutely," Motley said with a smile. "I've seen the IQ scores. You were the best model of your year. You're a rarity—expensive *and* elite. Not many parents could afford a Fourteen. I wasn't surprised to hear that your father's the packet chief." He paused.

"Not so good at talking, though," he added with a touch of remorse. "When it comes to that, Fourteens are easy to outsmart."

"What?" Martin asked. But Motley didn't stay to explain. With one quick movement, he was on the platform.

Martin looked around, startled. The children were gone. Motley was at the controls now, and the packet car was rolling into the loading bay. Martin ran after it, but his father grabbed him. "You'll spring the net," he said.

Motley reappeared in the open doorway of the car, his handsome face regretful. "Good-bye, Fourteen!" he called. Then bells rang, and the steel gates swung open. The packet car got away.

CHAPTER EIGHT

The transmitter arrived a couple of hours later on a special flatbed packet car, looking like a white enameled freezer that had sprouted an ugly growth of red wires and short metal segments. The freight bots knew not to go near it. Fat and ungainly, it lumbered off the packet, extending for the purpose a series of thick gray cylinders. Laboriously, it climbed the corrugated support framework of the steel gates, using a number of squat, clawlike legs. Once it reached the high ceiling, the transmitter wedged itself tightly between two I beams. There it brooded, watching over the suburb like a spider watching over its web.

Dad observed the transmitter's sluggish progress, trying without much success not to look repulsed. But Martin missed its arrival. He was spending the remainder of Rest Day shut up in his room, trying to make sense of Cassie's departure. Over and over, he played out the episode with the red packet car, looking for the precise moment when he should have made his move, as if he were studying a game cartridge to unlock the next level. Unfortunately for Martin, real life refused to grant him game saves, but he was so unfamiliar with deep regret that it took time for this realization to soak in.

At the next morning's playing of the national anthem, the family was quiet and withdrawn. Mom and Dad voted for opposing sides, but today Mom didn't try to argue Dad over to her point of view. Dad didn't disappear from the house, but he didn't speak, either. He sat like a lump at the breakfast table, holding his coffee but not bothering to drink it.

Martin stirred his cereal as Cassie would have done, staring into the colorful bowl as if he could hypnotize himself into believing that his little sister held the spoon. The doorbell rang about the time the cereal turned gray.

Principal Thomasson stood outside with a small flock of frightened students. "Martin, you're not ready," she observed.

Martin glanced at his pajamas and then at her. "Ready for what?" he asked blankly.

"For school," she replied in a chilly tone. "Students get walked to school in orderly groups, remember? I live on your street. I'm walking you to school. I'll give you five minutes to get ready." She transferred her gimlet glare to Chip, who stood by his side. "And leave your dog at home!"

For once, Martin welcomed the soporific routine of the school day. It occupied him without requiring his full attention, and it gave him something to do. Every now and then, the frustration of Cassie's departure would flare up inside him, and he could feel himself glow with the heat of it, like a steaming iron. But that happened less and less often as the endless questions trickled by, cooling him off with their impassive demands.

At recess, he stood with the others in rows on the playground, singing songs from the latest commercials. Last week, he had been a champion of the tiny and defenseless. This week, he felt unimportant, puny compared to the older students, uninteresting to the rest.

"Martin, you weren't singing," said Mr. Ramsey sharply. "You can lead this next one, then. Give us the Tic-Tac-Taco jingle: 'I'm a Mexican jumping frijole.'"

School ended. Martin tagged submissively home in Principal Thomasson's flock, with no little hand nestled in his. He found Mom sitting at the kitchen table looking at the family's photo modules. Her eyes were swollen from crying, and her hair was a tangled mess. What looked at first like a craft project turned out to be a dozen crumpled tissues.

"Hey, son," she murmured, attempting a smile. Martin came around the table and gave her a hug. "I've missed you," she said. "How was school today?"

Martin could think of no word bland enough to describe the experience. "It was school," he said at last.

"I wonder how Cassie's doing," Mom said. "Do you think her school is far away? I wonder what they're learning." It was the first time Martin had heard an adult mention the children since their departure, and something that had been building up inside him deflated with a sigh of relief. All day, he hadn't mentioned the Wonder Babies because he wasn't sure if it was allowed. He hadn't known how much longer he could stand it.

"Maybe they're learning about isotopes," he said. "Cassie was working on a lecture."

"Was she? Tell me about it," Mom said. So Martin sat down at the kitchen table and explained what he remembered of half-lives and fission, not very clear on the processes but happy in the memories, while Mom played the cooker and chose their dinner—two lemons and a bell: chicken-fried steak.

But Dad came home and spoiled everything. "I wouldn't talk like that," he cautioned. "The walls."

Mom looked stunned. "But this isn't like the others," she said. "Cassie wasn't removed from the suburb. She's at school."

He shrugged. "Better to be safe."

They sat down to dinner, but Mom was too upset to eat. She rinsed her food down the drain. "Walt," she said in a small voice, standing at the sink, "I don't think I can bear it, not talking about her. I miss her. I have to have *something*."

Dad came to put an arm around her. "You have so much, Tris," he said. "Cake decorating, stained glass, judo. You'll get through this. How did the chess club go today?"

Mom pulled back and stared at him. "I didn't go to the meeting," she said.

"No?" He looked uncomfortable. "I'd rather you'd gone. This isn't the time for . . . unless you were watching television, eh?" He smiled the way he always did for photos. "I'll bet that's what you did."

Mom looked completely baffled, and more than a little ill. "Do you—" Her voice shook. She paused to bring it under control. "Do you have any idea what's going on here? She's gone, Walt. Gone! How can you stand there and smile? And you didn't even—" She choked and stopped, shaking her head.

"Didn't what?" Dad asked.

Say good-bye to her, thought Martin, watching them. That's it—I'm out of here. And he left the room, called Chip, and curled up on the sofa with his dog. The raucous noise of a skateball game drowned out his parents in the kitchen. This was one conversation he didn't want to hear.

A short while later, Dad came into the room, looking unhappy, and settled down in his recliner. Martin expected his mother to join them, but it appeared that she had gone to bed.

Jell-O, the furniture for every taste, prattled the television. *A bright new look for your living room, just as soft as the real thing. Matching sofa, love seat, and ottoman come in black cherry, orange, strawberry, blue raspberry, and green apple. Jell-O furniture—the sweet suite!*

Martin idly watched the commercial. Just a few years back, the Wonder Baby ads had been on. Maybe there'd been ads for his model. He tried to think what a commercial for him might say. Had they mentioned his special aptitude for action game cartridges? When he and David played a game, he always got the highest score.

Maybe he and David had been different brands, like soft drinks. But just because a new soft drink came out, the old ones didn't go away. Why had that happened when the Wonder Babies came out? How did that work?

"Dad," he said, "I want to know about babies. Like the year David and I came out. I mean, where did we come from?"

Dad gazed at the television. "Good question, son," he said. Then he didn't say anything else for some time.

No one but you wants to watch the big game? asked the television. *Break out Hey, Where's My Dip?—the talking chip bowl! Up-to-the-second wireless feed tells your bowl who's out and who's down. Simple voice programming sets it to root for your favorite team. Shout along together as you share popcorn or chips. Hey, Where's My Dip? By the makers of the Drinking Buddy coaster.*

"It happens something like this," Dad said. "A girl grows up and becomes a woman. She wants to experience the miracle of life. So she finds a man and settles down to get married, because you can't have a baby unless you're married. The regulations are very strict about that."

"Oh yeah?" Martin said, a little uncomfortable. This didn't seem to have much to do with commercials.

"That's right," his father said. "So she gets married, and she and her husband save their pennies, and they file the right forms, and when the forms get lost, they file them again. And before you know it, the stork comes along with just the baby they wanted."

"Like me."

"Not exactly like you," Dad said. "Your mom was different. For most women, once is enough, and then they swear, never again. But with your mother, she forgot everything the minute she held you. She just had to go through it again. All the other mothers said she was crazy, but she went right ahead and did it anyway."

"Hey, I get it," said Martin. "It's painful having a baby, right?"

"Painful? I'll say! The paperwork is unbelievable! Having one baby takes months of forms. A woman can sit at her television console for an hour every morning. But when you come back and want another one, it's *years* of forms this time, everything from your blood type to your shoe size. And if the first baby cost a pretty penny, you'd better sell the family scooter to pay for the second one. We're still paying on Cassie. I hope they give us a refund. Having children is painful, all right!"

A refund! Martin felt queasy. "But you wanted her, right? Didn't the stork bring Cassie? What *is* a stork, anyway?"

"That's a special packet," Dad said. "Pure white paint, climate-controlled, with a little incubator crib inside. I'll get a message on the console: 'Stork under way for Mr. and Mrs. So-and-So,' and they'll come down to the bay to meet their newborn. Just as cute as it can be, the stork packet is." He sighed. "We haven't seen the stork around here in years."

The next morning, Principal Thomasson rang the doorbell, and Martin fell into ranks and trudged off. Mr. Ramsey paced and stared out the window while the students worked. No classroom lecture popped up on his monitor to bring even the imitation of human contact to the schoolroom. The building was as lifeless and silent as a meat locker.

When Martin got home, Mom was more like her old self, painting a watercolor picture at the kitchen table. Martin glanced at the painting: pink and purple, a face with golden curls.

"How was school?" Mom asked.

Martin shook his head. The bare reminder of the day robbed him of speech. He found one of Cassie's juice boxes in the refrigerator. "I'm glad she's out of there," he said, stabbing in the straw.

"What do you think she's doing now?" Mom asked.

Martin heard Chip whining in his bedroom, but he sat down at the kitchen table. "I bet she's sitting on a rug somewhere, reading a new module," he said. "I bet she'll sit there for the next five hours."

Mom laughed. "I hope she's doing . . . math," she said. "She always did love math." Then she caught her breath and wiped her eyes.

Martin jumped up from his chair. "Better go let out the dog."

"Sure," Mom said. "Son, don't mention this to your dad."

"Yeah, I know," said Martin.

The rest of the week limped by, a dismal round of school and television. Soon Mom was looking brisk again, but Martin couldn't feel better. Whether he was sitting in the living room or standing on the playground, he couldn't help noticing how the place had changed. It wasn't just Cassie; an entire range of small faces and young voices was gone. The suburb felt different and dull, like a soda left out to go flat.

On the evening of Workday Five, Martin sat in his beanbag chair, wondering what he would do with himself on the weekend. He wasn't supposed to go anywhere, and he was sick of television. Chip lay beside him on the rug, muzzle on paws. The poor dog wasn't having a good week either. Martin was so concerned about his modified status showing up during the inspection that he had ordered Chip to spend almost all his time "sleeping."

"Dad's home," Mom called.

And that meant dinner, Martin thought. At least eating was something to do.

"I wish you'd come home on time," Mom was telling Dad as Martin walked into the living room. "You almost missed the speech about tomorrow's vote. You know I hate having to explain them to you."

"Tris!" Dad said. "I never miss the President's speeches!" His glance flickered over to the listening walls.

"What? Oh! Right. Sorry, dear, just a little joke. Of course you're always home by six o'clock."

They stood in a hungry and impatient little knot, waiting for their leader to speak. Patriotic music and a waving flag replaced a toothpaste commercial: *The glitter in our toothpaste puts the sparkle in your smile!* Then the President faced them across his large uncluttered desk.

"Fellow citizens," he said, looking sadly at them out of the television screen, "today I entrust to you a problem that wrings my very heart. Unscrupulous product developers have unleashed upon us a model of child incompatible with our way of life. The so-called Wonder Babies, marketed to unsuspecting parents as 'new and improved' infants, have developed a disturbing liability record. They cannot be taught, and they cannot be led. They will tear apart the fabric of our culture."

Mom took two steps backward and sat down on the couch. The color drained out of her face.

"What I must propose will sadden you, as it saddens me," the President continued. "But I know my people: you will act bravely and wisely. Vote tomorrow morning against preserving this unsafe product line, so that I may know I have your support when I initiate, as I must, an orderly removal and replacement process."

His sober face gave way to a body-painting commercial, and the three of them turned and made their way into the kitchen. There they sat like so much extra furniture while the minutes ticked by.

It was Dad who recovered first. He fetched the ravioli from the cooker and spooned it onto their plates. Out of habit, Martin started to eat. Dad was eating too. Mom hadn't moved.

"I don't get it," Martin said, spearing a plump piece of pasta and wiping it against his plate to get rid of the sauce.

Dad flashed him a warning look and nodded toward Mom. "Let's not discuss it, son. It's upsetting."

Mom didn't seem to grasp the fact that they were talking

about her. The pain and bewilderment in her eyes alarmed Martin. Dad leaned toward her and gave her a little shake. "Tris, how about some dinner?"

Mom pushed her chair back and left the kitchen, walking as if she were asleep. They heard her footsteps dragging down the hall. Then they heard her bedroom door shut.

Dad sighed and drummed his fingers for a few awkward seconds. Then he spooned another helping of ravioli. "Eat up, son," he said. "No sense letting good food go to waste."

When the national anthem blared from the speakers the next morning, Martin was already awake. He had eaten two bowls of chocolate cereal to pass the time. Dad had taken a brisk walk in the bright spring morning. Mom hadn't yet left her room. Dad sent Martin to knock on the door.

"Time to vote," he called.

Mom stumbled out, wearing a pale blue bathrobe, her long hair looped about untidily. A pattern of bedsheet wrinkles had embossed red lines into her puffy face. Martin hadn't known his mother could look so old.

They waited in silence through the solemn parade of patriotic footage for the television screen to turn to input mode. Martin found himself hoping that maybe today it wouldn't happen. But at precisely seven twenty, the screen blinked its readiness for their votes, just as it did every day.

REMOVE WONDER BABY PRODUCT LINE FROM SUBURBS, read the vote screen. YES OR NO.

Dad stepped forward, grim and resolute. YES, he voted. Mom stumbled forward, so pale that her face was tinged yellow. Her vote was also YES. Martin barged between them to stare at the screen. It couldn't be true.

"What is going on here?" he cried.

"Martin!" said his father sternly, hustling him over to the couch. "Martin, we are not going to discuss this."

Now a wave of heat was pouring through Martin, sweeping him along on its tide. "Not discuss?" he demanded from his seat on the couch. "You just voted to get rid of Cassie! And now you're—what?—gonna walk in and sit down to breakfast? Just like everything's fine? Are you *nuts*?!"

"It's the best of a bad situation, son," his father said, bending over him, that earnest, comfortable face peering into his. "It's not a question of how we feel. This is a public record. There's nothing we can do about your sister."

"Nothing you can do?" Martin repeated. "Vote no! That's what you can do!"

His mother's face, swollen and tear-streaked, appeared over his father's shoulder. "It doesn't matter, Martin," she said sadly. "Do you think they're going to give her back?"

Martin's eyes stung now, and his parents' faces wavered like toys under the bathwater. "It does matter!" he wailed. "You sent her away—*my* little sister! And I didn't want her to go, and I told you, I tried to warn you, but you wouldn't listen to me. And you both voted—you *both* voted . . . You've never both voted the same way in your life!"

This struck him as hilarious, and he couldn't stop laughing while the faces of his mother and father flickered to and fro. Then a new face appeared, a black muzzle and worried brown eyes, and a heavy, furry weight crawled onto his lap.

"They got rid of her, Chip," he whispered, holding the dog tightly. He hid his wet face in Chip's tickly ruff. "They got rid of my little sister, if you can believe it. They just—poof!—just gave her away."

"Martin, think," Dad said. "The President's right. She wasn't happy. Now she's in a special school made just for them, where they can all be together."

It was Mom's turn to laugh. "Oh, the special school!" she said, and her voice was soft and bitter. "'Just think how happy they'll be in their nice special school.' It was brilliant, wasn't it? Suckered me right in. Do me a favor, Walt. Give it a rest."

At seven thirty, the President's face filled the screen. He looked as somber as he had the night before. "Good morning, my friends, my citizens," he intoned. "We meet on an historic occasion. Once again, you lift from me the unbearable burden of statecraft and give me the benefit of your heroic resolve. The people have spoken. You want the Wonder Babies removed."

"My poor daughter," whispered Mom, staggering to the couch and dropping down beside Martin.

"To those of you who have suffered the most from these fraudulent claims, I pledge that all of those responsible will pay. You dissatisfied parents will have the opportunity to test out a new product that will restore to you the joy of parenthood. It will guarantee that no one loses out during this transitional phase as regulators work to bring the stork program back into compliance."

The screen faded to black and came back up in soft hues of pastel. Little children ran and played at a park, their exquisite faces relayed in gentle close-ups.

Childhood, said a quiet voice. *Because you want to be needed. You deserve to be loved. Childhood. Have the child you've always wanted. Each Childhood model is as special as you are, as unique as your hopes and dreams. Choose from options like* clever *or* lively, shy *or* bold, *to create a Childhood model just for you.*

"It's a toy!" cried Martin.

Images of infants in pale pink and powder blue were floating across the screen.

Cherish your very own Childhood baby. Nurture her as she grows. Will he be an early walker or a late bloomer? It's up to you to decide. Do you have a favorite age? Your Childhood model will always be that age. Childhood. For the parent in all of us.

"That's sick," declared Martin, getting up from the couch. "Replacing Cassie with some stupid toy!"

"I think it's a wonderful invention," said Dad, settling down in his recliner. "It gives people the experience for a fraction of the cost and brings parenthood within everyone's grasp."

"It's sick!" repeated Martin. "Mom?" But Mom had shuffled back to her room. Martin threw himself down on the floor and started putting on his sneakers. "I'm going over to David's," he announced.

"Not today, you're not," Dad said, changing the channel. "You're not going outside unless you've been invited to play in Mr. Ramsey's tournament. You'll sit right down on this couch and enjoy your television."

Martin hurled his sneakers across the living room floor. They hit Mom's craft cabinet with a bang. "Oh, *great,* Dad, because I just *looove* television! I just can't get enough! That's what we kids love more than anything. We want to buy every little thing we see!"

Dad glared at him and snapped the recliner upright. "This is not the time for foolishness!"

"No, no, no, I mean it!" Martin hopped up and danced over to the wall. "Orange drinks and monogrammed handbags, rainbow gumdrops, personalized pencil launchers!" He located a sequin and talked into it as if it were a microphone. "Rings to match my eyes! Eyes to match my rings! I—want—it—A-L-L!"

"Martin, that's enough!" shouted his father, jumping up. "Go to your room this minute!"

"Okaaay," yodeled Martin. "I've got cool stuff there, too. No television, but I've got all fourteen game cartridges from the Make-a-Mutant Battle Machines House-to-House Hunt-Down series. Only $17.95," he called to the sequin as his father marched him off down the hall. "Don't forget—kids love 'em!"

Martin stewed in his room for a couple of hours, alternately fuming and playing his game cartridges. Then he went into Cassie's bedroom. Everything there was still exactly as it had been when they had left to meet the red packet. Her bed was unmade, with dolls scattered about in various stages of undress, and her big bunny smiled at him from the corner. He picked it up and went looking for Mom.

Mom wasn't in her bedroom. Martin found her in the living room. She was sitting on the sofa in her blue bathrobe, watching the game shows. Martin glanced away quickly from the contestant on the screen.

"Hey," he said, "that Motley guy didn't have us pack any clothes for Cassie. Isn't that weird? You'd think she'd need a toothbrush."

Mom didn't answer. She just stared at the screen. *You've*

chosen Column Four, Dissimilar Metals, the television told her seriously.

"And she left her bunny behind," Martin went on. "You know she can't sleep without her bunny. Do you think there's some way we could send it to her?"

Mom still didn't answer, but after a few seconds, her jaw began to quiver. Then spasms shook her shoulders, and she snatched a sofa pillow to hide her face. Sobs wracked her frame—long agonized rattles and wheezes of air. They seemed about to shake her apart.

Martin watched her in stunned horror. Then he raced to the door and bolted from the house.

No one was outside today, washing a scooter or playing tag. They were all inside watching television. Martin crossed the street and made his way into the deserted park. Shoeless, he ran across its green gravel, looking for a place of peace and safety.

The play structures drew him like a magnet. So often he'd taken Cassie here while Mom finished an art project or went to a class. Just two weeks ago, he had joined Cassie on the swings.

It was ironic that the part of the suburb devoted to its youngest members should have the greatest feeling of age. Nothing new had been added here in decades. The structures had faded from once-bright primary colors to more mellow shades. What had been yellow was now soft maize, and what had been blue had lightened to the color of a well-washed pair of jeans. There was a comfortable shabbiness to the play structures, a kind of genteel and venerable poverty. Perhaps that was why Martin loved them. He rambled among the swings, slides, logrollers, chain walls, teeter-totters, and twisted tubes of tunnels. They were abandoned now, strangely still and motionless, missing the little children as much as he did.

Chip trotted up, carrying Cassie's stuffed bunny, and deposited it at Martin's feet. Martin picked up the toy and patted its stuffing into place. A wave of weariness broke over him, and he realized that he was trembling. He didn't know what to do or where to go.

The tallest tube slide loomed above him. "She always made me follow her up," he murmured to Chip. "She was always afraid she was gonna fall." He reached for the handholds and footholds carved into the ladder panel and clambered up to the crow's nest at the top. He sat down in a corner of the cherry-colored shelter, away from the partial walls of slide and ladder. No one could see him from the ground, and all he could see, high overhead, was the powder blue ceiling and yellow skylights of the steel dome.

After a minute, Chip's pricked ears and black-and-tan face appeared at the ladder opening. He scrambled in to join Martin. "That was a pretty good trick," Martin said. "I wish I'd been on the ground to see it." The shepherd lay down beside him, and Martin curled up, resting his head on thick fur. He hugged Cassie's bunny to his chest.

"They're never gonna talk about her again, Chip," he said. "I could put money on that. One day I'll come home, and her room will be something else, like a craft room or a place to put Dad's bowling trophies. Everything that belonged there will be gone, just like my best pair of jeans and my favorite jacket. It'll be just like they threw her away." His chest began to ache with misery.

"Pretty soon, I won't be able to come here anymore. This park is gonna be full of little bot brats, all circuits and gel. Dad'll buy

Mom one even if she doesn't want it, and pretty soon she'll be cooing and singing. And all Cassie's pictures will disappear out of the photo modules." The lump in his throat choked him off.

The truth about his future sank down on him like a steel plate, crushing the life out of him. Boring school. Boring television. A home that wasn't home anymore. "I hate this!" he cried out. "I'm going crazy here. I can't live anymore in a place that—" But then he saw the sequin. White and glassy, it shone like a tiny flashbulb against the cherry-colored panel. Even in the park, the walls had ears.

"Oh, forget it. I'm going to sleep," he muttered, turning his face away from the sequin. "That's all I can do for the rest of my life, just sleep." Chip's fuzzy coat tickled his nose, but the rise and fall of the dog's breath was soothing. Now, why would they make bots breathe? Martin wondered as he dozed off.

At first, his dreams were a tangle of nonsense, mirroring the chaos in his thoughts. Then he became aware that he was walking through a golden haze. This is what blowing sand looks like, he thought. I'm outside, and that's what's outside—nothing but blowing sand.

Then the golden vapor changed hues to lavender and silver. Bright particles clung to his clothes. Chip came up beside him, his fur coated with the stuff, all creamy lilac and white, like whipped cake frosting.

"Hey, Chip, this isn't sand," he said. "It's body glitter! I think it's fun to be out here." But even in his sleep, he knew this couldn't be right. Why put windows in a packet that rolled through glitter?

The glitter swirled away like steam off coffee, and an extraordinary landscape emerged. Great tumbled translucent cubes of gel in every conceivable color stretched as far as the eye could see. He was standing on a broad soft cherry-colored slab that bounced like a trampoline. It's Jell-O! he thought. Now I finally know what's outside! Light shone deep into the gel, so that his slab looked like a crimson pool, and the stacks of multi-colored cubes glowed like stained glass.

Children were running and climbing on the slabs, jumping off the stacks and bouncing back up like superballs. But the children weren't gel, they were real. The Wonder Babies were shouting and playing, having fun now that they were outside.

"I've gotta find Cassie," he told his lavender dog. "Cassie must be here. She saw all of this. She sat by the window." He ran toward the Wonder Babies, bouncing higher and higher, whirring through the air like Granny's birds. There was no limit to how high he could go. There was nothing out here to stop him.

Someone scrubbed his face with a wet rag, and he opened his eyes. Chip was there, licking his cheek, plain brown and black again. Beyond Chip, the steel dome closed over the suburb like a lid, cutting him off from the outside. But he could feel it out there waiting for him: a colorful wonderland where dreams came true.

"Hey, Chip," he said, sitting up. "I've got the craziest idea."

CHAPTER NINE

That afternoon, the transmitter crawled laboriously down the wall of the loading bay and left on the back of a flatbed packet to Central. Weary with relief, the packet chief watched it leave. Then he went from block to block to spread the word that the inspection was over. Soon the streets were full of suburbanites gossiping with neighbors, working on their lawns, or playing H-O-R-S-E around the basketball hoops. Mr. Ramsey called an end to the baseball tournament in the sixth inning and went home to catch up on his rest.

Matt and David showed up on Martin's doorstep.

"Listen, we have a problem," David said. "The ImCity cartridge won't play. Well, it will, but the screen's black, and you can hear stuff moving around and making weird noises, but you can't see anything."

"Maybe it's nighttime in the game, and they've knocked out the lights," suggested Martin.

David shook his head. "I changed the clock."

"Then it sounds like the monsters have taken control and set the game palette to six straight zeros," said Martin. "I think you'll have to throw that cartridge away."

"Six whats?" Matt asked.

"Crap!" David said. "That was the best game yet. So, what are you doing? Wanna hang out?"

"Can't," Martin answered. "I'm busy."

"Doing what?" Matt asked. David punched him on the arm. "Hey, you wanna know too!"

"We'll help you," David said. "Come on, Matt." And they started to step inside.

Martin put out an arm to bar their way. "Let's see the bugs first." They pulled purple chips from various pockets, and Martin led them back to his room.

"Whatcha working on?" demanded David, looking around. "Your cartridges aren't even on."

"This isn't a game. It's real," Martin said. "Let's say you're going somewhere, a place where there aren't any cookers or fridges. And you're going to be gone—I don't know—maybe a few days. What do you bring?"

"Oh, that's boring," David said, throwing himself onto the bed. "That's a little kid's game. Where's to go?"

"No, I'm serious," Martin said. "It's a drill, like in the Survivor module of House-to-House. What if our suburb got invaded and we all had to escape in packets? It could happen." He piled up school supplies on his desk. "Okay, here's my backpack, all cleaned out. What do I need?"

"A toothbrush?" Matt suggested. David groaned.

"No, that's good," Martin said, and he retrieved it. His friends looked shocked.

"Your dad hasn't heard something, has he?" David asked. "Like, they're closing off our air vents or something?"

Martin shrugged. "I just want to be ready."

By dinnertime, they had loaded his Hi-beam, a bar of soap (over David's strenuous protests), a tube of antibacterial cream ("in case someone gets shot"), his toothbrush, three rolls of toilet paper, and a jumbo pack of double-pop gum, the last because they all really liked it. They scrounged through the pantry, sampling as they went, in search of energy bars that didn't also happen to taste horrible. Mom stocked energy bars by the dozens. They filled the backpack with acceptable varieties until it was bulging.

"Something to drink's more important than food," David opined. "Our bodies are mostly water. You can eat all the garbage you want and still keel over in a couple of days."

"Yeah, you slosh when you walk," Matt jeered.

"Oh yeah? You stink when you fart," David snickered.

"No, David's right," Martin said. "I need to think about water." Once again, his friends stared at him in awe.

"Are they sending, like, commandos or something?" David asked humbly.

"The walls have ears," Martin said, looking grave.

They raided the pantry again, this time returning to Martin's room with six gallon-size juice bottles held together by webbing at their caps. It took two of them to hoist the load.

"Put it on the dog," David said. "He's tough." So they called over Chip, who had been keeping a cautious distance from Martin's friends. They laid a velour couch blanket across Chip's back to act as padding and slung the connected juice bottles over that, three bottles on each side. Martin found one of Cassie's kneesocks and an old cloth belt to tie the bottles in place.

"If your life depends on an Alldog," David remarked, "you better bring his reset chip, too. Those modules can freeze up, you know. Cinder did once, and I didn't know about it. I just thought she was sleeping for a week."

"She froze because you stuck a joy buzzer on her," Matt said.

"Yeah, but I still thought she was sleeping."

Martin dug the reset chip out of the box under his bed and put it into his backpack. He hefted it in satisfaction, thinking of the bright Jell-O fields. Then he unhitched Chip and let the bottles slide to the floor. He was ready for anything now.

"You'll tell us if they're coming to get us, right?" Matt asked.

"Yeah," David said. "Promise you'll tell us what's going on. We're your best friends."

"Sure," Martin said, and he decided that he would. First, he would go outside and see if it was safe. Then maybe he would bring them something he found. And if he decided he was leaving for good, he would say good-bye. They wouldn't believe him, of course. They'd probably laugh. But later, they could tell all the others.

Martin couldn't sleep that night for excitement. At four o'clock in the morning, he crept out of the house and ran to the loading bay, ready to begin his research. The big freight bots crowded around as if he were going to issue them orders. They didn't seem to comprehend the idea of day or night, weekday or weekend.

"Okay, here's the deal," he told Chip, ignoring them. "I know it's still dark out there, but I want you to go check it out. Find out if I can live outside this dome, if the air and stuff are okay. When you've made up your mind, taken readings or whatever, then bring me back something that means yes or no. If it's a mouthful of sand, well, then I'll know I can't live. Or a rock. That's bad news. But if you bring me . . ." Here, his mind went blank. "I don't know what you should bring me. Just be sure I know it when I see it."

Ears pricked, Chip surveyed him steadily, and Martin gave

his thick ruff a grateful pat. Even if he couldn't explain things very well, this was a dog who knew what to do.

Martin didn't watch the bizarre transformation of German shepherd into packet car. Ever since Chip's last change, he had had nightmares in which his dog dripped and ran like melting ice cream. Instead, he wandered over to his father's console and tapped a key to bring up the screen.

SUBURB HM1 ONLINE, he typed in just for fun. After a few seconds, the line moved up as an answer came in.

SUBURB BNBRX ONLINE GOOD MORNING WALTER

Martin was elated. Man, this guy never sleeps! he thought.

SUBURB HM1 ONLINE HI FRED HOPE YOUR WIFE DIDNT DIE IN THE NIGHT

The line blinked at him for a moment. Then it moved up.

SUBURB BNBRX ONLINE I PREFER TO KEEP OUR EXCHANGE PROFESSIONAL

Martin hooted with delight.

Alarm bells rang. Chip came rolling through the big gates, looking terribly strange, and Martin quickly looked away. After a few seconds, the shepherd came up to him, normal again.

Martin dropped to his knees to stroke the dog's ears. "Well? What did you find out?"

Chip laid something limp on the concrete in front of him, and Martin picked it up warily. It was a few inches long, with narrow green leaves, like a very thin, jagged head of lettuce. One end was a round starburst of soft yellow spikes. Martin turned it upright and recognized it.

"A flower! Just like the daffodils on Mr. LaRue's window!"

A little round creature climbed down from the yellow flower

and crawled onto his hand. It was bright red, with a black head and black spots, and it had the tiniest black feet Martin had ever seen. "A bug!" he breathed. "A real bug!" It was beautiful.

Unexpectedly, the bug's back split into two sections, and it took off in a gentle whir. It could fly, just like a toy airplane. Martin watched it with shining eyes.

"I'm going out there, Chip," he said excitedly. "Right now! I don't care if it's still dark." But he didn't. Instead, he scurried for cover behind a stack of cardboard boxes. "Chip, hide!" he whispered to his puzzled dog, and in another second, the bot was by his side.

Someone had called the elevator.

Martin heard it grind slowly up its shaft and halt at the suburb level. After a short pause, its wheels began turning, and it came humming down. Dad walked out into the loading bay. He was wearing his black suit with a white shirt and thin black tie. It was the outfit he wore to funerals, and seeing it unnerved Martin. Had someone in the suburb died?

Dad could have been the body. His face was dead white and waxy, and his gray eyes looked black. Martin was worried that he might find the joking comment on his console, but he didn't walk over to check. Instead, he stood in the middle of the loading bay, hands clasped, staring straight ahead of him at nothing.

A minute or two later, the alarm bells sounded again, and a packet car rolled in. It, too, was somber black, but it was much larger than a funeral packet. No windows interrupted the simplicity of its sleek lines, but a door at the back slid open. Dad walked up the steps and went inside.

A man's voice rang out, hearty and welcoming. "Mr. Glass!

I'm sorry to have interrupted your night's sleep. Please, take this comfortable chair across from Truth, and we'll get started."

Martin heard his father speak, but he couldn't make out the words. Drawn by curiosity, he found a hiding place closer to the packet.

"We were quite pleased," the man was saying, "with the results of the inspection. Overall, you've got a very nice suburb. A few anomalies here and there, but nothing we can't cope with."

"Extend your hands," interrupted a woman's voice. It sounded flat and toneless. Martin heard his father give a cry of pain.

"Now, now, Glass," the man said with a chuckle. "Truth just wants to hold hands! The stinging will stop once the probes find their places. Truth, how are things going?"

"Ready to begin," the woman said.

"Good," said the man. "As I was saying, this is a fine suburb. One of my best. People aren't spending all of their income just at the moment, but I can always count on them to support new product lines. There's just one problem from the inspection that we need your help with, Mr. Glass. Where did you hide those children?"

"The—the children?" stammered Martin's father, his voice high with fear. "They were in school. That's what I heard. Every one. Zero absentees."

"True," declared Truth.

"That's not what I'm talking about," the man cut in. "I mean, where are the other children? The Wonder Baby product line. You put them where the sensors couldn't pick them up, and that's a serious offense."

"No, no!" Dad protested. "No, they were collected. You sent a packet for them last Rest Day."

"True," the woman said.

"Collected?" The man sounded suspicious. "Tell me how this happened."

"A special car came, with a collector adjusted to deal with children," said Dad's trembling voice. "He talked about the inspection and invoked the Wonder Baby recall. I knew we had to get rid of the product, so I cooperated completely."

"True," agreed Truth.

Martin didn't wait to hear the rest. It all made too much sense. His father's odd absences in the evening: Dad couldn't bring himself to look Cassie in the face. Motley's stern warning: *I expect your full support.* The collector bot had come, and Dad had pretended everything was fine.

Martin abandoned his hiding place and took the elevator out of the bay. He didn't care whether they heard him or not. He didn't care about anything. He walked home through the shadowy streets as the first gray hint of dawn lit the skylights. He didn't run this time. There was nowhere to run. The truth lodged inside him like a red-hot blade, and it would be there for the rest of his life. His little sister had been sent away to die. There was no special school, and Dad had known it.

He turned on all the lights in the house, looking for his mother, and found her asleep in Cassie's bed. "Mom," he whispered, kneeling by her side. She rolled over and opened her bloodshot eyes, and her puffy face was blotched and stained with grief.

"Mom, I get it," he said. "I know why you watch the game shows."

She sat up and hugged him fiercely, and he felt her tears falling onto his neck, but he couldn't run away from this, either. "You think she's still alive," he said as calmly as he could. "That's why you watch them."

"I don't know," Mom sobbed. "Maybe. Probably. They always do something with them."

"Then I'm leaving," Martin said. "I'm going to go get her out of there. I promised her I would."

His mother pulled away to look at him in wonder. "No one can live outside!"

"It's a lie," Martin whispered, casting a glance at the listening walls. "There are things living out there right now. Flowers, Mom. Real ones. I've seen it! I'm not coming back till I've got Cassie."

"I've always hated it here," Mom said, and her voice was taut with emotion. "I've tried my best to find things to do, but this is no life. If there's a way—any kind of life for you out there—then you take it, Martin. And I don't see how, but I hope you find your sister. If you do, don't ever bring her back here."

"Don't worry. I'm not good in school, but I always know the stuff that matters." She smiled through her tears and nodded, as if these were things she didn't need to be told. "And tell Dad—" What? he thought. That I hate him for being a coward and a liar? That I never want to see him again? "Tell Dad good-bye."

Martin made Chip lie down so that he could saddle the dog with the blanket and bottles of juice. He grabbed his backpack and scooped out some energy bars to make room for Cassie's stuffed bunny. Then he left the house. But he stopped at the sidewalk.

"Dad isn't supposed to be at work yet," he told Chip. "I bet he's coming home to vote and eat breakfast. And I don't know what I'd do if I saw him right now—punch him or something—so we have to not meet him, not up here, not in the loading bay. Which way can we go?"

Martin was facing the park. Without thinking, he was scanning its familiar sights: the play structures, the jogging track, and the distant ball field. A small, dignified building near the street caught his attention. Its sides were faced with polished gray stone, and its wide asphalt walkway was lined with ornate street lamps, but the big metal door was shut. Martin had never seen it open.

"The entrance to the factory!" he said. "Bug got through that door, and that means we can too. We'll go through the dark place under the streets, the underground way, and Dad'll never see us."

The first few joggers were out beating the pavement as he and Chip crossed the street to the park, but he told Chip to unlock the long-disused building. "Don't worry about anyone spotting you," he said. "We won't be around long enough for them to catch us."

The door opened easily, as if it were used everyday. Wide marble steps lay at their feet, and Martin could see the black granite panels of the lobby below them. Chip trotted down the stairs, his load of juice bottles swinging, and Martin turned to close the door. "That's it for me," he said as it shut out the view of the park. "No more suburb."

They made their way from the factory lobby into the darkness underground, with its concrete pillars and strange whispering noises. "I wish David and Matt could have seen this," Martin muttered as he played his Hi-beam over its mysterious conduits. "But it's too late for that now. And too late to say good-bye."

Eyes aglow, Chip led them to the door marked AUTHORIZED ENTRANCE ONLY, and from there, they tiptoed to the loading bay. Martin peeked in at the large space. The lights were still on, but the ominous black packet car was gone. So was Dad, home no doubt for breakfast before beginning the workday in earnest. Had his father noticed the lights, the joke on the console? Either way, it no longer mattered.

He couldn't ignore his pet's transformation this time, made even stranger by the load of bottles. In order not to loosen the ties, Chip couldn't flatten out like a table, so he became long and thin, a playground riding toy with legs that arched out from wide shoulders like a swing-set frame. Strangest of all, this mechanical construction still had a dog's head, which swiveled around to watch him as he scrambled astride, trying to avoid the uncomfortable bottles. Hand pegs and foot pegs jutted out to assist him. "Chip, that's gross!" said Martin.

The bot dog shifted forward. Martin's heart gave a leap. This is it, he thought. Time to try my luck in a new world. The steel gates opened, and the one-of-a-kind packet car rolled through.

The washing room past the loading bay was damp and gloomy. Martin heard water dripping loudly into a drain. Then they were in a long dark curving corridor that seemed to last forever.

"Chip, hurry up!" Martin urged. "I can hear something banging in here!" But the banging noise was only Martin's pounding heart.

A further set of gates opened, and light flooded in, a stark contrast to the dim corridor. Chip stopped rolling. Martin stumbled off, blinking, his eyes smarting from the glare.

The first thing he saw was his own sneakers, standing in white and black gravel. Next to them, springing out of the rocks, was one of those yellow starburst flowers surrounded by jagged green leaves. Martin bent down to look at it, delighted. Then he looked up again, amazed. A veritable carpet of those flowers stretched around him.

He stood next to the rails, but they no longer ran on concrete. Now they ran on a narrow gravel road, with crossbeams of thick dark wood. No houses were here outside the suburb, but he saw metal sheds and buildings, and not too far away was a high concrete-block fence. The whole thing could have been under the steel dome, except for those heartwarming yellow flowers that sprang up everywhere out of the hard-packed ground.

"So we're out, but we're not out, is that it?" Martin mused. Then a huge shadow fell over them. Martin looked up and discovered for the first time what the word *outside* meant.

Clouds were sweeping by overhead, not painted white blotches on a ceiling, but living, moving creations of tremendous variety and grandeur. They were all shades of pink and purple, and they were all sizes as well. Some were tiny rags that tore quickly along; others were great fluffy masses that coalesced and transformed in a slow, graceful progression of dignity and beauty. Martin stared, slack-jawed, unaware of the passage of time. Never in his life had he seen a sky that changed.

"What are you doing out here, young fellow? We've got to get you home!" And a click at Martin's wrist signaled that he was a prisoner.

CHAPTER TEN

Even Chip's surreal transformations hadn't prepared Martin for the sight before him now. An older model of bot, it didn't have enough simulation gel to appear entirely human. Most of it was a typical steel-bodied freight bot, with a wide cylindrical base and many telescoping arms. One of the arms had caught Martin's wrist in a tight-fitting pincer clip.

A man's face smiled broadly from atop this mechanical creation. It was ghastly to see a living human head sprouting from a heap of metal, but then, this head didn't exactly seem human. It looked like the head off one of Cassie's little fashion dolls, the kind that came with its own tennis outfit.

"It's dangerous for you to be out here, young man," the head admonished. "We'd better get you back where you belong."

"Let go!" cried Martin. He tried to pull his hand free of the machine's grip, but his muscles were no match for the hydraulics in a bot's arm.

"Back to safety," insisted the smiling bot, dragging him along as it rolled up the gravel incline by the packet rails. "Look both ways," it advised before it advanced onto the tracks. "We wouldn't want anything bad to happen to you."

"Chip!" yelled Martin in despair.

He thought his problems had doubled when his other hand was seized and a smaller twin of the security bot locked its pincer tightly around his wrist. This doll-headed bot only came up to his waist, but it smiled at him just as nauseatingly. Then he noticed that it had six big juice bottles slung, gunslinger-style, around its middle, and a folded green blanket draped around its neck.

The little twin spoke to its senior colleague in vibrating data-transfer speech, and the big security bot released Martin's wrist. "My partner is looking after you," it announced in its friendly way. "Be safe!" It rolled off out of sight around the corner of a shed.

In another second, Martin's wrist was loose, and Chip was Chip once more. "Good *dog*!" Martin said, dropping to his knees to hug the bot. Chip was wagging proudly. "Man, am I glad I don't own a real dog! You are such a cool pet. Let's get out of here before any more of those guys show up. That thing's gonna give me nightmares."

He and Chip quickly covered the distance to the concrete fence. There, the rails were blocked by a big gate of sheet metal. Chip stopped and barked sharply. Then he cautiously stepped over to the rails and froze into a wheeled playground toy again. This didn't seem so creepy after the security bot.

"I get it," Martin said. "There's another alarm here." He climbed on, and they rolled forward. The big steel gate trundled off to the side to let them through, past the limits and controls of the world that Martin had always known.

"Wow!" he whispered. "Wow!" he exclaimed. "Wow-hoo-yahoo-whee!" he cried at the top of his lungs, scrambling off the rolling dog in excitement.

It was the distance that fascinated him first. After a lifetime of living with a steel ceiling and a concrete floor, the vastness of the living landscape was like a drug. He stood on the top of a hill, a concept he had known before only from sandbox games, but this hill was an enormous thing, and the ground fell gradually from it for a long, long way. The ground below the hill wasn't flat either. It undulated, rising in curves and falling in scoops. Off to his left, high hills like a fence seemed ready to blockade the clouds themselves.

The colors out here were as unlike those in the suburb as they could possibly be. Ranging from tawny brown to dark olive, with every shade in between, the land coordinated beautifully with itself. And the early-morning sky, all tints of red, pink, indigo, and gray, seemed a marvel of perfect choices. These were not bright, garish, plastic colors, but soft, friendly tones. Martin's orange shirt and electric blue backpack screamed "bad taste" by comparison.

Chip blended in beautifully. The mystery of the shepherd's elaborate black-and-tan decorating scheme was solved at last. It was a shame that the handsome beast had to carry the load of juice bottles around. Their labels—even worse, their contents— were a positive riot of artificial colors.

The sun attracted Martin next. He barely knew it for what it was. In class, they had studied the solar system, but they had never learned how these astronomical bodies appeared from the surface of their world. In the suburb, the sun brought light through the translucent skylights. But it never revealed itself as he saw it now, an enormous egg-yolk ball low on the horizon, filling the world with a golden red glow. Its power dizzied him, made him want to run and shout, pushed him along just as surely as the blind rush of wind that flattened itself against him and blew his hair into his eyes for the very first time in his life.

"Let's go!" Martin yelled, and he ran down the hill. He ran and ran, tripping over stones and dodging through the knee-high flowers and leaves, catching his jeans on stiff plants that crackled and sprang back. The wind poured over him, cooling the sweat from his brow, and he jumped and ran and shouted, sure that he could run forever. Then the backpack got heavy and clumsy. It bounced around on his shoulders. He stopped and felt a stitch in his side.

"I'd be all the way—across the suburb by now," he wheezed to Chip as he stood with his hands on his knees. "I couldn't go—anywhere—but back. Here, I can go forever! Who thought it would be so *big*?!" And he joyfully tackled the shepherd, causing bottles and blanket to slide about in an alarming fashion.

"The national anthem's playing right now," he noted with satisfaction, sitting down in a group of pink wildflowers that sprinkled yellow dust all over his blue jeans. "Out here, it's quiet. No television."

But that didn't mean it was silent. Fluted cries were beginning to sound across the open field, by ones and by twos. Small forms were whirring through the air overhead, black against the sun. Birds! Martin recognized them from the springtime tape played over the neighborhood loudspeakers and from his grandmother's tales of those creatures like soft bundled socks. "You were right, Granny," he whispered, shivering with pleasure. "Everything you told me was true."

The light grew brighter every second. Now Martin noticed small noises joining the birdcalls and the rustling of plants: faint buzzes and clicks and other busy sounds. He realized that the dusty ground was alive with movement. Bugs of every make and model were marching, crawling, springing, and flying off in all directions.

"Chip!" he called. "There's bugs everywhere! What David and Matt wouldn't give to see this!"

While the suburbanites under the steel dome cast their votes that morning, Martin spent an ecstatic half hour collecting and cataloging bugs. He didn't know their names, so he gave them names of his own: Superman (able to leap houses in a single bound), which came in both a green and a yellow model; and the Copycats, who followed one another everywhere in long lines. For one type, he found not the bug itself, but only its big outer hull, translucent and almost weightless, so he named this one the Ghost Bug. And then there was the bug that waited quietly, with folded hands and solemn demeanor, until some happy little bug came close enough for it to pounce on. These, sad to say, he named the Teachers.

A steady mechanical clacking distracted him. Some distance away, looking like a toy, a packet car moved along the rails. It grew steadily in size as it came toward the suburb, and Martin crouched ineffectively in the tall weeds as it passed by. It wasn't a scary black packet, but a regular merchandise shipment. Still, it reminded Martin why he was outside.

"Okay, no more fooling around," he told Chip. "This is gonna be easy. Cassie left in a packet, so we'll follow the packet line. It'll lead us right to her."

They walked along in the open field, keeping the packet line in sight. The day grew warm and exceptionally bright, and Martin's backpack straps began to hurt where they rubbed his shoulders. But he had a million new things to see. Several times that morning, he spotted animals crossing the fields nearby. Two had long ears like Cassie's stuffed bunny. One looked like a thin dog. And even the things he had already seen, like the clouds, seemed to change form and color every minute.

It was noon when they came to a stand of trees about fifty feet away from the packet rails, which were running through the fields on a steep-sided, raised road of gravel about ten feet high. The trees straggled down a nearby ridge and spilled into the field, like a crowd of people who had followed two or three leaders.

Martin stood in their shade, put his hands into the ribs of their bark, and felt wonder deep in his heart. They were not tall and powerful like the I beams that ribbed the steel dome, but their branches swayed, and their leaves rustled in the wind. He could tell that they were alive.

By the afternoon, he began to feel uncomfortable. His skin had flushed pink, and he felt thirsty and feverish. He was happy when they came to a shallow creek in the valley floor. The packet rails crossed it on a long iron span, but he waded right into it and bathed his sore arms and face in the cool water.

"Chip, come look at his!" he called. "Fish! Just like in the pond at the park! But these are really teeny, and they all swim the same direction, like they're having a parade."

When evening came, a glorious view spread out around him. In a shallow valley, a large sheet of water shone like a mirror in the glow of the sinking sun. Beyond it rose the dark wall of the high, high hills, a band of shadowy giants. Thousands and thousands of birds wheeled and cried in the air above the lake, their shapes stark silhouettes against the golden light, and the sunset sent yellow and purple streamers of cloud halfway across the sky.

Martin sat down and watched the brilliant show for as long as it lasted. He couldn't look away for a second. He stared at the huge crimson ball of the sun itself until black spots danced before his eyes.

Worn out by the glory he had witnessed, Martin was unprepared for the stars. They were like a surprise planned by an overly indulgent parent. "This is *too* much, really," he confided to his dog as the brilliant lights clustered in the heavens. "I never thought a place could look like this." It grew cold, and he unslung the bottles from Chip, wrapping the blanket around himself and cuddling up to the dog. It didn't occur to him to seek shelter. From day to night and from summer to winter, life in the suburb changed very little.

An almost full moon crept into sight over the gravel embankment beside him. "What next?" he said drowsily. "I swear, you gotta be watching this place every second." But he fell asleep in spite of his own advice.

He awoke in the half-light of dawn to a very different scene. The morning was very cold, and his blanket was wet and clammy. A chilly wind whipped down from the distant peaks. Chip's fuzzy bulk protected Martin as well as it could, but Martin still felt as if the wind blew straight through them both.

Worst of all was the pain from his skin.

Patches of it were burning in agony on his face, his ears, the back of his neck, and all the way down his arms. Even in the dim light, he could see that those arms were deep, flaming red. When he turned up the short sleeves on his T-shirt, he could see a sharp line of demarcation, normal above and damaged below. There was no doubt about the cause: it was the sunlight.

"Oh no!" he said. "Chip, maybe they're right. Maybe humans can't take it out here." He pressed a finger gingerly into the scarlet skin and watched it leave a stark white print that slowly flushed red again. "Man! I sure don't want to die!"

As the hours passed, he hiked along in pain, miserable with a feverish thirst that the lukewarm, syrupy juice couldn't slake. He had a limited view of his surroundings because he was huddled under the shade of the velour blanket. When the sun rose higher, this became a fluffy walking sweatbox, but Martin was too afraid of the brilliant sunlight to risk laying it aside. Hour by hour, he hoped that his skin would return to normal, but hour by hour, his suffering increased. The inflamed areas burned and itched by turns, but this was an itch that would tolerate no scratching.

This shouldn't be happening to him, he thought. This was a gorgeous place, a boy's paradise. He wanted to belong here, just like the birds and bugs did. It wasn't right for the sun to try to kill him like this. It just wasn't fair.

As they walked on into the late afternoon, Martin began to worry. Except for the occasional packet clattering by, he'd seen no sign of human life for two days, and the suburb was long out of sight. The size of this beautiful wilderness was exhausting him, and its toxic light was roasting him alive. The torture of his burns was constant and excruciating, and he ached like a victim of the flu.

"I don't know what to do," he told Chip. "I wish you could tell me. Should I go back? Is it already too late to go back? Am I just going to feel this way until I die?"

They came to a wide field with a stream down the middle. A little knoll made a perfect spot to watch the sunset, and later they could climb down it and take shelter behind some rocks to escape the cold night winds. In the meantime, Martin bathed his burns in the stream and got a little relief from the pain. His red skin seemed thick, like a rubber mat.

He slept badly. He'd chosen the field because he enjoyed the sound of moving water, but other creatures seemed to like it too. Several times in the night, Chip bristled and growled, and Martin heard strange calls and noises. The audacity of his journey was beginning to eat at him too. If humans lived under domes, it was because they had to. He'd been stupid to race out into this world just because he had a toy that could unlock doors.

When the sun rose, Martin didn't rise with it. The strain of the last few days had worn him down, and his pain had abated somewhat, so that he finally felt almost comfortable. Warmed by the rays of the sun, he drifted in and out of dreams. At last, he rolled over and opened his eyes.

Chip was looking at him. No, not looking, he thought, puzzled, as he scratched his itchy arms. Chip was staring at him, even analyzing him. A stab of pain stopped his scratching. He glanced down and shrieked.

His arms were thickly covered with large, clear blisters. His scratching had broken some open, and underneath was not skin, but the gooey flesh inside him. Martin gingerly felt his face and found on it the same horrible condition. There was no question now about what was happening to him. His contaminated skin was coming off.

"Oh no! Oh no!" he moaned, holding his head in his hands. "I can't live without skin. I'll rot away! What am I gonna do?"

He was too distraught to formulate a new plan, so he kept to the plan he had. He followed the packet lines, holding the blanket over his injured body as he had the day before. Ironically, he felt better today. The pain wasn't as intense. But every time he looked down at his arms, he could see that he was doomed.

Around midday, he faced a new problem. At the top of a high hill, the packet lines split. One set of tracks went off to the left, and the other continued straight ahead. This possibility had never occurred to him.

The hill seemed worrisome for other reasons. Several huge, dish-shaped structures stood high on stilts at its apex, and cylinders the height of a person stood near the packet line junction. Martin didn't know what they were, but Chip seemed afraid of them. The shepherd nipped the belt loop at the back of his jeans and held on.

"Okay, okay, I get it," Martin told him. "I'm not going over there. Let's head around the side of the hill to see where these lines go."

Crouching behind bushes, they crawled around the right side of the hill and studied the packet line that went straight. It headed off into more country like the land they had already explored. Crossing that line cautiously, they studied the line that went to the left. Off in the distance, they could see a steel dome shining with almost blinding brilliance in the noonday sun.

Martin sat down right where he was, and his dog, sensing trouble, crouched down close enough, bottles and all, to lay his big head in Martin's lap. "It's like this, Chip," Martin said. "I don't think Cassie's in there. I mean, how could she be when the Exponents got voted out of the suburbs? But I'm not going to be able to find her now. I'm dying. I mean, really dying! And it's"—he gulped—"it's kind of scary; you know, like your reset chip is for you. So I want to go there. They can just give me the shot, so I don't have to wait around till my fingernails fall off."

Chip's brown eyes gazed adoringly up at him, and the long bushy tail whipped from side to side. Martin stroked Chip's thick fur in silence for a little while, grateful to have a friend.

They arrived at the suburb yard in the middle of the afternoon. Martin didn't feel too bad, but his blisters were starting to break and leak who-knew-what onto his clothes. He took off his backpack and untied Chip's juice-bottle harness.

"This is good-bye," he said huskily, and he knelt down to hug his dog. "I don't want you going in with me. They're gonna put me in the hospice room, they won't let a dog in there, and then they'll load me up in the funeral packet and send me away. If you go in, they'll try to reset you to program you for some other kid, and then they'll find all your special chips. That'll be it for you. We'll both be gone."

Chip whined in protest, rolling on the ground and kicking his feet in the air. Martin felt terrible.

"Look at you, you belong out here," he said. "You match the place. I want to think of you out here where they can't get you. I want to know you're where I wish I was, running around loose."

But Chip remained inconsolable. He howled with grief. Martin couldn't help crying along with him. "It's for the best," he said, giving the dog a last hug and laying his face against the rough fur. "Stay outside and don't follow me. That's an order. But look, when you see the packet coming to get my body, then you'll know it's all over. Then you can do what you want. Now, come open this gate for me."

The sheet-metal gate rolled out of the way, and Martin walked into the compound alone, trying to ignore the high-pitched yelps of the forlorn dog outside. A doll-headed monster of a security bot welcomed him with smiling concern and escorted him into the building.

"Washing facility," announced the bot as they came through the room just outside the loading bay. "But that's for packets. You're not a packet. You shouldn't be washed here. I don't know if you should be washed at all. Maybe it isn't safe."

"I take showers all the time," Martin muttered. His heart was in his toes.

"I wouldn't recommend it. You don't look waterproof," the bot said in a friendly way. "I inspect the packets when they come in, and I know about fragile loads. You must be fragile. You're encased in bubble wrap."

"I'm not— Oh, never mind."

The security bot activated an override, and the steel gates opened to let them in. Martin looked at the sickly fluorescent lighting, the dull gray concrete, the ceiling and walls hemming him in. I'm home, he thought gloomily. Why did they make these places so alike?

But there was one difference that struck him painfully: his father wasn't sitting on the high stool behind the console. A short man came forward, somewhat older than Dad, with nondescript hazel eyes, light hair mixed with gray, and anxiety stamped upon his round face. When he drew close enough to see Martin clearly, his face blanched with dread and pity.

"Holy smokes, young man!" he cried. "What in blazes happened to you?"

"I'm dying," Martin blurted out, and the man didn't contradict him.

"You stand right there, right where you are," he said, crossing back to the console. "I'm calling Social to bring you medical aid right now. You have to go into the quarantine room immediately. Tell me your name, and I'll send word to your parents. I'm not up on you youngsters like I could be. I'm afraid I don't recognize you—not right at the moment, anyway."

"I'm not from here," Martin said. "I'm from HM1. I'm Martin, the son of the packet chief there—you must know him: Walter Glass."

"You don't say!" The short man came out from behind the console to study him again. "I guess I can't blame you, running away from a father like that."

"You know about him then," said Martin, miserable at the thought of his father's cowardice.

"I've worked with Walt for years," said the man. "My name is Fred Buckalew. Welcome to BNBRX. I'm sorry; I'm not allowed to shake your hand for fear of contagion. We'll get you to the quarantine room, and Alice will be along soon to help your . . . um . . . condition. Go on ahead and I'll direct you. Don't touch anything. Turn around and head down that hallway there to your left."

Martin walked along in a daze. "So *you're* Fred of BNBRX," he confirmed. For some reason, this didn't seem to fit.

"I'm sorry I said that about your dad," he heard the packet chief say behind him. "I shouldn't have talked badly about a colleague. Walter Glass is a little different, but that's his business. In the fourteen years we've worked together, he's never once let me down." They came to a door that slid out of the way at Martin's approach. "And a right turn here."

Martin walked down the narrow hallway, the confined space making him more depressed than ever. "I guess you didn't care for Dad's efforts to make friends, huh?" he muttered.

"Your dad tried to make friends?" Fred asked doubtfully. "Okay, stand right there and I'll buzz you in."

The quarantine room didn't offer much privacy. The entire wall facing the hallway was made up of glass panels held by metal framing. Inside, the color scheme was white and sterile. There was a vinyl-covered bed and a couple of molded plastic chairs. Metal cabinets lined the walls, leaving room for one narrow door in the back corner. A large television, set into the wall and protected by a clear plastic panel, displayed peaceful images from what Martin and his friends called the "geezer channel."

Standing about twenty feet away, Fred pressed a switch, and one glass panel slid aside. Martin stepped through, and the panel shut and sealed behind him. Once inside, he felt funny, thinking of the rats in Motley's refrigerator. Fred came to the other side of the glass now, closer than he had dared to come before.

"Alice will be here any minute," he said, his voice tinny as it came through the speaker system. "Can I get you anything in the meantime?"

Martin realized he was ravenous. "I've been eating snack bars for three days. Can I get some real food?"

"Sure," Fred said. "There's a cooker inside the cabinet over there, and a little fridge next to that. Let me know if the fridge isn't stocked, but I think it is; we've been paying extra attention to it lately." He excused himself to return to the loading bay.

Five minutes later, the cooker had dished out a tasty bowl of chicken broth followed by a serving of vanilla pudding. Martin sat down on the vinyl-covered bed and wolfed down the meal. Then he pulled the cooker handle and tried for other foods, but he had no luck. The cooker was set to stop at this combination. That was fine as far as it went, but it left him feeling unsatisfied.

Alice turned out to be a plump, grandmotherly woman with faded blue eyes and short dry flyaway hair that didn't look as if it should be that shade of brassy blond. She smiled reassuringly at him through the glass, and her face had what Cassie called "happy wrinkles," the kind that come from a lifetime of smiling. He watched her unload items from a cloth bag she had brought and set them into a cabinet next to the glass wall.

"Hello, Martin," she said through the intercom. "I'll unlock this cabinet in just a minute so that you can pull these things out from your side. I want you to take these pajamas and this medicated soap and go shower with cool water. Use the soap for your face and hair, too. Don't scrub your hair like normal because you have blisters on your scalp. Just work the soap in and then gently rinse it. And be very careful when you dry off with the towel. Pat, don't rub. If you rub, you'll take off skin, and that's going to hurt."

"Pat, don't rub," Martin muttered. "Got it."

"Now, did you get any bites while you were out there? Do you have itchy or infected areas anywhere? Yes? Maybe? Then dab them with this medicine before you put on the pajamas, but don't put it on your burns, even if they itch. And if you find any insects sticking to you after you take off your clothes, don't worry. Just hold this jar over each one and press the button on the side. After a few seconds, the insect should drop off into the jar. Check yourself all over—that's what the full-length mirror in there is for. Then, when you're finished, drop the jar down the special trash tube. And drop your clothes down the clothes chute. The chutes are labeled. Don't get them mixed up."

Martin collected the items from the cabinet. He had expected a dying boy returning to his people to be treated with a little more dignity. He certainly hadn't expected a lecture on soap and towels. He sorted the items she had put into the cabinet. Then he opened the door to the bathroom and found himself staring into the full-length mirror.

The face that stared back was so appalling that he couldn't make a sound at first. He could only look at himself in wide-eyed panic. Far up into his hair, his skin was gruesomely discolored, dark red and dark brown, scabbed and crusted, with blisters piled upon blisters.

He shrieked and ran back into the quarantine room. "I'm gonna die, I'm gonna die," he moaned, hugging himself and collapsing onto the floor. "Please, just please give me the shot now."

"Honey, what's wrong?" asked Alice's tinny voice.

"Look at me!" sobbed Martin. He glanced over his shoulder to peek at his grisly reflection again. Tears were running down his distorted face now, zigzagging around the blisters and scabs.

"Your skin? Honey, you'll be all right. That's just a sunlamp burn." Alice was smiling kindly at him through the glass. "I've had sunlamp burns myself. When I was a girl, there was this craze for the things. They were supposed to make us pale people have nice golden skin, but five extra minutes under one, and we wound up looking like you."

"But how can you live through this? What happens next?" demanded Martin. "How do you get new skin?"

"Oh, the burned skin peels off, and the new skin is a little bit darker. Each time under the sunlamp, we could take it a little longer. Some people got to where they really had golden skin, but most of us just kept burning and peeling. They recalled those lamps as unsafe."

"Then—then I'm not gonna die? Well, then—crap!—what am I doing here, anyway?"

"Go shower," Alice said firmly. "Remember: pat, don't rub. And brush your teeth with the toothpaste in the cabinet over the sink."

Martin was so furious with himself that he couldn't even enjoy the reprieve he had been given, much less the chance to feel clean. Cassie was out there somewhere, and he had no idea what danger she might be facing. Meanwhile, the minute he had a few little blisters, he was ready to cash it in. Why hadn't he noticed that he was already feeling better? Why hadn't he waited to get well on his own?

He emerged from the bathroom to find that Alice had put a pillow and sheets into the cabinet. "Time to rest," she said. "You'll have to make your own bed, sweetie. I wish I could do it for you. Look at you! You look much better already. You'll be your old self in no time."

"But see, here's the deal," he said, sitting down on the vinyl bed. "I'm not staying here tonight."

"Of course you are," she said. "You can't go back to your house tonight, you have to give the medicine time to work. You're very lucky that you weren't outside for more than a few minutes. Otherwise, who knows what would have happened to you?"

"A few minutes?" he repeated in surprise. "No, you've got it all wrong."

Fred hurried up at that moment and switched off the intercom. Then he talked urgently to Alice. As he did so, her face lost its happy wrinkles. Frowns don't look right on her, Martin thought.

When the intercom switched off, the sound on the geezer channel came back on. *Your family may not want to mention your bad breath,* the television advised Martin soberly.

Fred hit the switch again. "Martin, a packet is coming tomorrow morning to take you home to your family," he said. In spite of this good news, his voice sounded edgy. In fact, he hardly looked like the same sympathetic man who had met Martin in the loading bay. "In the meantime, you're to stay in here and recuperate. You'll want to be looking your best for your mom and dad, won't you?" His smile didn't reach his eyes.

"But that's just it. I don't want to go back," Martin said. "No need to order up a packet. Just let me back out the way I came in." Alice and Fred made no move, so Martin pushed on the sliding panel. It didn't budge. This place is all about locked doors, he reminded himself, glancing down. But no friendly dog stood next to him. He had left Chip outside.

For several seconds, he stood there, refusing to believe what had happened. He was locked in. Helpless. Trapped! All he needed was Chip, but Chip wasn't coming. He had specifically told him not to.

Alice and Fred were having an argument now, and Alice was shaking her head. "It's the only safe way!" the packet chief was saying. "This is dangerous, I tell you. There's no knowing what nonsense he might blurt out."

"He's too young," Alice declared. "Too light. That gas is formulated for adults. I don't know what it might do to him."

"Hey, guys?" Martin said in a small voice, and they looked at him, startled. Fred muttered something about the intercom switch.

"What is it, dear?" Alice asked. The kind look was back in her eyes.

"I forgot something outside," he told her. "A toy. My Alldog. And—and I can't sleep without my dog," he said, wretched over having to tell such an embarrassing lie. "I'm really uncomfortable and scared without my family. Couldn't you please send a freight bot outside to get me my toy?"

"Oh, you poor thing," Alice said. "I'm so sorry for you! Of course we'll fetch your toy for you, won't we, Fred? We'll do it right away."

The packet chief was watching Martin through narrowed eyes. "Absolutely not," he said.

"But, Fred!" she protested. "Surely a harmless little toy—"

"—isn't harmless," Fred cut in. "It's modified, isn't it?" he added knowingly to Martin. "And that's how you got out."

"Well, n-no," Martin stammered, but he felt his face betray him.

"You see what we're dealing with," Fred told Alice. "He's a

loaded gun. There's no telling what he'll say or do. He could cost us our jobs, endanger the whole suburb. Now will you put in the code to turn on the gas?"

"It's wrong to gas a child," Alice said.

Martin remembered what Dad had said about Bug: *Social took him down to quarantine and gassed him for me, so there'll be no trouble tomorrow.* That was what Fred wanted when Martin's packet came.

"Alice," he pleaded, coming up to her at the window, "please don't let him turn on the gas. I want to know what's happening, and I won't cause trouble. You know I'm not a bad kid. I've done everything you told me to."

"You see, he even knows about the gas," Fred said. "He's been through this before."

Alice ignored the packet chief. "You poor dear," she said warmly to Martin. "I'm sure this is all a misunderstanding. You get some rest now and don't worry about a thing. I'll be back to check on you in the morning."

"No, you won't," Fred told her. "I'm supposed to station freight bots to blockade this hallway. It's off-limits until his packet arrives."

"Oh my goodness!" said Alice, looking shocked.

"I don't get it," Martin said angrily. "I'm not some kind of criminal. I should be a hero, that's what, and get interviewed on television. I'm the only person in this whole place who's ever gone outside. Don't you even want to know what it's like?"

Alice's face changed color from pink to deep red and then to white again. "Oh!" she gasped. "Oh, Fred, I never thought! I—" And she turned and scuttled off down the hallway.

"No, we don't want to hear any of your wild tales," Fred said grimly. "I'm switching off this intercom and locking it off, just in case someone manages to sneak in here. If there's anything you need, better ask for it now. I'm very sorry, I don't like being harsh, but I warn you, I'll put up with no foolishness."

Martin was so upset that he was afraid he might start to cry. He thought about the mess he was in and how he had gotten there. Dejected, he sat down on one of the chairs. "You told my dad about me, right?"

"Yes."

"And—well, what did he say? Was he worried? Did he say he was sorry?" He studied his pajamas. They had a blue and yellow Night Fighters pattern on them, and he was sure they made him look like a moron. He felt his eyes begin to sting.

There was a pause, and he glanced up to find Fred looking uncomfortable. "Oh, he pretty much said what he always says," he answered.

"Well, then—wait a minute. My dad says lots of things. I don't get what you mean."

Fred shrugged. "Walt said that he appreciates my concern, but he prefers to keep our relationship professional. I'm really sorry," he added, and this time he looked like he meant it. "But you know how your father is."

"Walt?" Martin said, bewildered. "You mean my dad?" He forgot that he wanted to cry. "Hold on," he said. "My dad never talks like that. You're the one who talks like that."

"Me?" said the puzzled man. "No . . ."

"Dad complains about it all the time," continued Martin in a rush. "We even make a game of it sometimes. Like the other day,

Dad teased you right before the black packet came in, maybe about five in the morning. He said he hoped your wife hadn't died in the night, and you said what you always say."

"I don't know what you're talking about," Fred said. "I've never known that man to make a joke. And besides, I never work that early in the day."

"So you've never spoken to my dad," Martin said. "Never once. Who do you guys talk to, then? And—hey, wait a minute! Then who's sending out that packet to get me?"

Fred stared at Martin in amazement. Then his face closed up like a clenched fist. "I knew you were trouble the minute I saw you!" he growled, and he snapped off the intercom and walked away.

The first thing Martin did after Fred left was order up four bowls of warm vanilla pudding from the cooker. He ate them rapidly, one after the other, before they could cool off. *I didn't think I needed to take iron anymore,* confided a lady on the television. Martin turned his back on her.

Now, he thought as he slurped the sweet stuff off his spoon, that guy Motley said I always know what's worth knowing. Okay, what do I know about what's going on now? What's going to happen next?

That special packet that's coming to get me isn't going to take me home.

Martin's skin prickled up into bumps. He didn't have to ask how he knew. He just knew. It was all in the way Fred had looked at him.

"Time to get out of here," he said, jumping to his feet.

The sliding glass panel, of course, refused to slide. He banged it, poked its rubber gasket, and pounded the wall nearby to hunt for hidden switches or panels. Nothing made it budge.

I'll have to break the glass, he decided. It's going to be a mess. He picked up one of the plastic chairs and hefted it a few times. Then, squinting, he hurled it at the panel. The chair bounced off with a bang and knocked back into Martin. He wasn't getting anywhere this way.

"Okay, what's heavy?" he wanted to know. Systematically, he made his way around the room. The bed wouldn't shift. The metal cabinets refused to leave their brackets. Nothing would break loose in the bathroom. Even the cooker and fridge were bolted down.

"Why is everything here driving me crazy?" he shouted. "I'll do it myself, then!" And he climbed onto the vinyl bed, took two running steps down its length, and hurled himself into the glass. A terrific jolt went through him, and a second later, he felt the back of his head smack into one of the chairs. The blisters scraped off his forearm as he slid in a jumble onto the floor. He climbed to his feet with pain shooting through him, so mad that he couldn't see.

Martin intended to coat the room with vanilla pudding. He meant to hurl bowl after bowl at those big glass panels until no one could see through them anymore. He pictured the thick goop dripping down the walls, splashing into the vents on the cooker, drying up and cracking into a hard yellow lacquer. Wouldn't Fred be disgusted! Wouldn't he be sorry he'd been such a jerk!

The first bowl was already cooking before Martin realized that Fred might be angry enough to order him into restraints.

Okay, bad idea. He didn't want to be handcuffed. But what a good time he would have had! He sat down on the floor to eat the pudding instead, regretting his change of heart.

Afternoons with Shelly, announced the television screen in elegant, free-flowing script. Shelly turned out to be a slow-moving heavyset sixty-year-old man with bulldog jowls and twinkling blue eyes. It seemed that Shelly had lots of friends in his neighborhood, and he was going on a walk to visit them. He was hoping that Martin would come along.

"Yuck!" said Martin. "Why can't old people take their own walks?" He spent a fruitless few minutes trying to find a way to change the channel, but the quarantine room television was permanently stuck on peaceful programming. Oh well, it could be worse. He could be watching game shows right now. Which brought him back to the problem at hand.

"Okay," he muttered to himself, wishing that Chip were there to listen, "let's assume I don't want to go where they're taking me, because I bet I don't. And let's assume I can't get myself out of here first, because I can't, and that's a fact. Now, what can I do? Fight when they get here? Not unless they send out someone my size."

A soft thump in the cabinet announced the return of his clean clothes from the laundry, and Martin gratefully changed out of the Night Fighters pajamas. I'll have to talk my way out, he decided, and I'm no good at talking. The Motley guy was right about that. But I've got till tomorrow to plan what to say. I better get to work.

So, while Shelly visited Gloria, who hadn't been feeling well yesterday; and Donna, who fed him pecan tarts; Martin ran through all the things that might happen the next day, over and over, like he was playing one of his cartridges.

But he couldn't prepare his heart for the shock it got the following morning when the glass panel finally slid open. In stepped a trim blond woman in a white lab coat and black slacks.

"Good morning," she said in a brisk voice. "You must be Martin Glass."

CHAPTER ELEVEN

Martin gaped at the woman, his mind echoing with Bug's screams. He felt exactly like one of those rats in Motley's refrigerator, with nowhere left to run.

"It's a pleasure to meet you, Martin," the woman said. Her eyes lit up with an obsessive glow, and she reached out to take his hand.

Wake up! called his brain. You thought of this. She's a bot! You know how simple bot programming is. Do something! Don't let her touch you!

"I'm not Martin!" he shrieked, jumping back. The bot woman paused, confused.

"Of course he is," said Fred, stepping into the room behind her. "That's the name he gave yesterday when he arrived."

"No, I'm not!" Martin yelped, positioning himself behind the vinyl bed. "I'm not Martin Glass. They're hiding him from you. I'll show you where he is."

Fred shrugged as the woman turned to him for clarification. "He's the person you've come to take away. I don't know why he's babbling like this."

"Liar!" Martin shouted. Okay, you worked on the Fred problem, he reminded himself. He paused to put his words in order. "That guy with you, Fred—he asked me all these questions. He wanted to know all this illegal stuff."

The packet chief's face went tight with anxiety. "Don't you tell her that!" he cried. "It's a lie. Tell her you lied, you little brat!"

"Liar!" Martin shouted in return. Between them, the bot woman stood still.

"Where is Martin Glass?" she asked. "I need to find him."

"I'll take you to him," Martin said, breathing hard, as though he were running a race. He pointed at the nervous packet chief. "And you. Stop talking about me and I'll stop talking about you."

The three of them walked down the hallway in silence while Martin's mind raced through more plans. He could take the woman to the school and pick out a kid who looked like him. Maybe there would be a crowd, and he could get away. Maybe he could push her out the elevator and ride it back down. He'd have to see what shaped up.

Another voice in his mind was whimpering with dread. You don't have a chance, it warned. You won't escape. All you'll do is buy a little time. There's no way out of this place.

They came to the loading bay, and Fred stepped to the console. It seemed to give him confidence. "All right, I've put up with enough," he said. "I'm the packet chief of this suburb, and I swear that's Martin Glass. Now get him out of here."

The woman swung her head to look at Martin again, and terror made him go weak at the knees. "No, they've hidden him in the school," he cried, backing away. "You're lucky I'm helping you find him."

"It's normal to be nervous," the woman said reassuringly, stepping toward him. "Many of my patients are uneasy about their journey. You *are* Martin, aren't you?" Her eyes lit up again. She looked like a child with a new toy.

Martin felt his hand seized in a tight grip, and he closed his eyes in a flurry of panic. But the hand didn't feel right. That is, it felt exactly right. It made him feel big and powerful again. He opened his eyes. Fred and the woman were several feet away, staring in amazement.

Holding his hand was a smaller replica of him.

"What is that doing here?" the woman demanded.

"I don't know," Fred said.

Just like him, the little Martin was wearing an orange T-shirt and blue jeans. It, too, was rail-thin and dark-haired. Its face held the same look of fear that he knew was on his own. It was even wearing his backpack.

But I'm not wearing a backpack, thought Martin, feeling muddled. It's outside with—

And then he knew.

From inside the blond woman came the vibrating sound of bot-to-bot communication. Martin's twin vibrated back, and the woman snapped around to face Fred.

"My colleague informs me that my patient is traveling to another suburb," she said angrily. "I'm to check your console for further orders. Why did you conceal this information from me? Why did you let my patient leave?"

"You're a bot!" Fred cried, astounded. "I never would have guessed! I don't have any idea what's going on today."

"Answer me, Packet Chief!" Her voice deepened to a roar. "WHERE IS MARTIN GLASS?"

"I thought he was the one in the quarantine room," Fred babbled. "Martin Glass, the big Martin Glass, not the little one. I don't know who—what—the little fellow is. Don't look at me like that! Ask them yourself. They're right here. No, where'd they go?"

Alarm bells interrupted him. The steel gates were opening. The woman let out a scream.

"My packet is leaving without me!"

Martin lay on his stomach inside the moving packet car, knocked flat by the jolt of their departure. His copy at the controls might have managed to get it moving, but he was hardly an expert driver. Martin braced his hands against the packet's open doorway to keep himself from sliding out. He had a perfect view of the loading bay he was leaving.

The bot woman threw herself after them in a mad dash to catch the escaping car. Martin wasn't worried. He remembered the day he had run after Granny's packet. The woman would trigger the air horn, just as he had done. Then the security system would catch her in its steel net.

But Martin had forgotten that she was a bot. She was chasing them down far faster than a normal woman could run. The horn went off in a heart-stopping blast, but the net dropped down seconds too late. He saw it fall right at her heels as she raced after them.

They rumbled through the dripping washroom, and the gates clanged to, shutting off the racket from the deafening horn. She tore down the middle of the tracks right behind the car, smiling brightly at him. "You *must* be Martin," she called over the clack of the rails. "Finally! I'm so glad. We're going to have a very good time on this trip. I've been looking forward to it."

Now they were in the long dark tunnel. The packet was picking up speed. Her lab coat flying, the woman was picking up speed too. The light flooding out from the packet's open door lit up her blurred legs, her cheerful expression. And all the time she ran, she talked to him.

"You'll be so excited to see where we're going, Martin. Many patients become so excited that they require sedation!"

They blasted out into the sunlight and careered past the metal sheds. Even though the packet car was doing its best, Martin could see that she was catching up. Her legs had morphed into something other than legs. They looked like wheels. And her gray eyes watched him like a missile locked on target.

The last security gate was coming up, but she was too close to the car for it to catch her. Do something now! Martin told himself. This is a bot. You know what to do.

"I'M NOT MARTIN!" he yelled as loud as he could. "MARTIN IS BACK THERE." And he lifted a finger from the floor to point toward the suburb.

Confusion crossed the woman's face, a flicker of hesitation. For an instant, she slackened her speed. As they whipped past the outer fence, the security net dropped over her and trapped her in a web of steel mesh.

They rolled away, and her struggling figure diminished in the distance. Martin thought he saw her mutate into strange forms, extruding waving tentacles through the net. Feeling ill, he closed his eyes and huddled on the floor, swaying from side to side with the movement of the car. It would be all right, he comforted himself. She could never squeeze her circuit board through the net.

Martin stayed on the floor, holding on for dear life, as they covered the miles back to the hilltop junction. When the car came to the T in the tracks, it turned in the direction that led away from HM1. His twin at the controls brought it to a stop.

"Chip, did you make us go this way?" The little boy shook his head. "So we weren't going home. I knew it!"

Before leaving, he took a quick look around the car. There was a small refrigerator filled with bottles of water and a cupboard containing snack-size bags of chips. Martin confiscated the supplies, laying them on a wide-bodied pink and yellow hospital gown and wadding it up into a makeshift bag.

At the front of the car, a big padded chair stood by the window. Leather manacles dangled from its arms and legs, and an IV bottle hung from a bracket. Martin fled out into the sunlight, afraid he was going to be sick.

His miniature self was gone. A gorgeous black-and-tan German shepherd frisked delightedly in the tall weeds, snapping at passing bees. "You computer chip!" cried Martin, attempting to gather the squirming dog into his arms. "You disobeyed me, didn't you? I told you to stay out here until . . . until the packet came for me. I get it! You saw this packet—you'd seen it before—you decided it was for me. And then you could be free to do what you wanted. Wow, Chip! You're too smart to be a dog, that's what you are."

Chip fell into his lap and whimpered with joy, licking the air around him. He realized the dog wasn't licking his face because of the blisters.

"Hey, I'm not dying either. This is just a little burn. It's gonna be gone in a couple of weeks." He held out his arms. "See? I'm looking better already." The blisters had gone down, but his skin was starting to peel off in thin, transparent sheets. "Isn't that gross, Chip?" he said, studying his arms with admiration. "I can't believe it all comes off like plastic wrap."

The day was wonderfully hot after the insipid climate of the suburb. Martin looked around at the shimmering landscape and felt his spirits lift. The myriad colors of wildflowers blended into a distant paleness, and the dusty shrubs and trees formed olive green smudges on the hills. He tilted back his head to take in the washed-out turquoise of the sky, the large birds that cruised lazily in circles.

"This is it, isn't it, Chip?" he said. "This is where we belong. We've got to get Cassie out here."

A clang behind him made him jump. The packet car that they had abandoned was rolling. "Did you set the brakes?" he asked Chip. Then he realized the packet was moving uphill.

The empty car gathered speed, rolling back the way they had come. It climbed the hill behind them that held those big scary dishes. Then it whipped around the junction in the tracks and headed toward Suburb BNBRX again, making excellent time.

"We could have been in there!" Martin whispered. "No way could we have jumped for it either. That means we've got maybe half an hour to get out of here before the freak in the lab coat comes after us." He remembered the chair inside her car and shuddered.

The surroundings didn't provide much shelter. There was nothing more concealing nearby than knee-high weeds. They scrambled through the wildflowers to a clump of scrubby bushes on a small knoll. Under these silver-leafed shrubs, they lay in the scratchy weeds, hiding until the bot's packet car went by.

About an hour after it had rolled away from them, the ominous windowed car came into sight. It rolled down the rails at normal speed, like any other packet. Soon it vanished in the distance.

Martin climbed out of the bushes and scratched the back of his blistered neck. "I think it's like this, Chip," he said. "If you're in their suburbs, they run your life, just like Bug said. If you aren't, they don't care. End of story."

He consolidated the supplies as best he could, tossing out a few of the worst flavors of bars to fit in as many bottles of water as possible. Although Cassie's bunny took up valuable space, he refused to throw it away; he was sure he would be giving it to her soon. He draped the shapeless hospital gown over his head and shoulders to cover his burns, tying it around his forehead so that it became a flapping desert burnoose. "How cool does *this* look?" he said proudly to his dog. It was just as well that Chip couldn't answer.

They followed the packet line away from HM1. The landscape around them offered little change: a series of rolling valleys continuing ahead, and the wall of high hills off to their left slowly drawing nearer. Only in the farthest distance could Martin see something different, something that was a deeper, brighter green, and then, just at sunset, a flash of brilliant light where he had seen none before.

"I bet Fred's message never got through to Dad," he told Chip. "I bet they'll never know what happens to us. And Mom and Dad—what do they talk about now that Cassie and me are gone? We're about all they ever used to talk about."

He imagined his parents sitting silently at the kitchen table. His heart ached, and even the beautiful sunset couldn't make it feel better. But Chip crept up close beside him and pushed his furry head underneath Martin's arm.

"You know what's a shame, Chip?" he murmured as he

watched the colors fade to indigo. "Mom would so love it out here. I've gotta find Cassie now. She's all I've got left."

Clouds moved in the next morning, bringing a cool breeze, and the sun stayed hidden behind a solid mat of gray. Light rain began to fall, the first Martin had ever encountered. He couldn't say that he liked it.

"Yesterday I was covered in plant dust, and today I'm covered in muck," he said as they slogged along through wet weeds. "I wish I was like you, Chip. You never get dirty." When a region of hair became grimy or tangled, the bot just resimulated it; patches of dirt slid off the regenerating hairs and fell right to the ground. But Martin didn't have this comfort. Soon his clothes were soaked, splashed with pale, gooey mud and plastered with wet plant bits.

When the rain ended, the sun didn't reappear. The day became warm and steamy. They came to a shallow lake caught in a wide, low canyon formed of rock laid down in long stripes of orange and taupe. Here and there on the lakeshore were large beige boulders, left behind from the weathering of the canyon walls. The rocks were still wet, and when Martin poked one with a stick, it scratched easily in a bright white streak. This was something Martin hadn't thought of: rocks could be soft or hard. He remembered his dream of the Jell-O landscape and wished it had been real.

He was out of sorts. He plunked a stone into the lake, watched its ripples die away, and then sat down on one of those soft rocks. It didn't feel particularly soft to sit on.

"I'm going to run out of water soon," he observed, taking off his backpack. "I guess I'll have to drink this lake stuff. And I don't know how much longer I can keep eating these disgusting bars. You're lucky you don't have to eat, Chip. Maybe starving is better."

A man in ragged cutoff jeans stepped from a nearby tangle of cattails, and Martin's heart nearly jumped out of his chest. "Quiet," the man commanded, holding up his hand. But he wasn't talking to Martin. He was facing Chip, who stood some twenty feet away down the lakeshore.

Martin couldn't see the man's face, but he saw his dog's reaction. Chip, too, had been caught completely by surprise. Now he crouched with tail and muzzle almost touching the ground, apparently too frightened to move.

"Hey!" Martin called. "What are you doing to my dog?"

"Just letting him know who's boss," said the stranger. "Out here, life is dangerous. You have to take charge."

He looked as if he would know what he was talking about. He was big and solid like a wrestler, the opposite of the soft suburbanites Martin knew. His sun-bleached hair was clipped into a short fuzz, and he was clean-shaven. His eyes were ice blue, startling in his darkly tanned face.

"It's hazardous to drink lake water unless you treat it," the man said. "So you're in danger of starving?"

"No," Martin said, backing away. "Well, yes and no. I guess I will eventually; I mean, if I haven't got where I'm going."

"There's a whole lake full of fish here!" said the stranger. "Eat one of them. Here, I'll show you how."

He pulled off a dull mustard yellow knapsack and began to take out equipment. His mottled gray-green T-shirt was so faded and stained that it was impossible to guess what color it had started out, and his sneakers had reached such a state of battered old age that it was obvious they would sink down, sighing, like two flat scooter tires the minute he took his feet out of them. By comparison, the tattered cutoffs looked relatively new. At least Martin could still identify them as a former pair of jeans.

Martin edged around him and ran to his dog. "Chip, are you okay?" he whispered. Shaking all over, Chip raised terrified eyes to his face. Then the dog laid his big head against Martin's knee.

"What's the problem?" demanded a voice in Martin's ear. The man stood right behind him, holding a fishing rod.

"You scared my dog!" Martin said angrily. Chip was trembling like the jelly he actually was.

The big man studied them with a puzzled frown. "Hey, I'm sorry," he said. "I just want to help. We'll try over here."

He scrambled onto a short bluff that overlooked the water, made his cast, and sat like a statue. Not three minutes later, the pole bent, and the man reeled in the line. A hand-size fish came up, shimmying from side to side. In spite of himself, Martin was impressed.

The man shook his head. "Too small." He expertly unhooked the shining creature and threw it back. Soon he had one twice that size on his hook, fighting to stay in the water.

"My dad fished in the park," Martin said, cautiously approaching, "but the fish would change into a number when you pulled them out—one, two, or three, depending on the size."

"I don't know how to cook a number."

The stranger removed the struggling trout from his line. He smacked its head against the ground, and the fish stopped fighting. "This one's small too," he said. "But big enough for you. Do you know how to build a fire?"

Suburb regulations strictly prohibited the sale of flammable devices. "What's a fire?" asked Martin.

The big man eyed him with something like disgusted pity and dropped the dead fish on the rock in front of him. "I'll be back," he said. "Watch out for the teeth; you can get nasty cuts from them." And he walked off, passing Chip, who shimmied like a trout to get out of his way.

In a surprisingly short amount of time, the man had kindled a fire, cleaned the fish, and cooked it in a lightweight skillet with a folding handle that he had produced from his capacious pack. "Here you go," he said, setting the hot pan on the rocky ground in front of Martin. "A fork." He brought out a flat fork with a shiny plastic handle. "Some salt." He produced a tiny square saltshaker and sprinkled the fish. "Now you're all set."

Martin ate ravenously. The lack of real cooking over the last several days made him ready to appreciate anything, but the fresh fish, barely out of the lake and right into his mouth, tasted blissful. He thought it was the best meal he had eaten in his life.

"Don't you want some?" he asked, but the man good-naturedly declined.

"I'm not hungry right now."

As soon as Martin was finished, the stranger took care of his camping gear, cleaning it and stowing it away. Martin watched, fascinated by his efficient movements. Chip crept up next to him, and he absently stroked the dog.

"Now that I've cooked for you," the man said, "you should tell me your name."

"I'm Martin Glass. I lived in HM1. That's the suburb down there." He waved a hand in the direction from which they had come.

"Martin." The man used sandy dirt from the top of one of the soft rocks to scrub a spot from his skillet. "Nice name. My name's Hertz."

"Like 'hurts people'?" asked Martin respectfully.

"No, I've never hurt people. It's a different kind of Hertz."

"Are you from a suburb?" Martin wanted to know.

"I don't like to talk about the past," Hertz said, fixing him with that ice blue stare. "I lost someone very important to me."

"Hey, I understand," Martin said. "I lost someone important too." And he told Hertz about Cassie. "I guess I should get going now. I don't know how far I'll have to travel."

"I'll walk with you," Hertz offered. "One direction is as good as another." Chip looked apprehensive at this, but Martin was glad.

They hiked through the open fields together and talked. Hertz knew an incredible amount of facts, from the names of insects, plants, and trees to the tracks and calls of animals. He told Martin that the high hills to the west were called *mountains* and described their snowstorms in winter.

"We had a snow globe in the living room," Martin said. "When you shook it, white snow flew around a little Santa Claus guy."

Hertz pondered this. "Maybe it was a terrarium that contained a mountainous or northern ecosystem."

"Well, it did have a teeny street sign that said *The North Pole*."

In late afternoon, they moved away from the packet line, heading toward a camping spot Hertz knew. Martin wasn't sorry to distance himself from the steel rails, where the bot woman traveled. On the other hand, they were his only clue to finding Cassie.

"I wish I knew where she was," he said. "I'm so worried about her. What if that Motley guy is on the other side of those mountains by now? Maybe I'm wasting my time."

Hertz grew thoughtful, and they walked in silence for several minutes. "Martin, I think you should ask about her," he said.

"Ask who? Do you have friends out here? Like, is there a whole group of you or something?"

"Sort of like that," Hertz said. "Don't you ever get the feeling that we're surrounded by forces we can't see?"

Martin slowly shook his head.

"Well, I know we are," Hertz said with that intense look of his. "Twice a day, I go up high and look at all the wonders of the world below me. And I seek guidance, and I find answers."

"You mean you figure out stuff?"

"It's not like that. Come with me next time. Then you'll see."

They had been heading, Martin realized, toward a high knob of ground. Over the next thirty minutes, they climbed it by the straightest path Hertz could find. Toward the end, it grew steep, and Martin needed help to scramble up. Chip slunk along behind them like a canine criminal.

The top was a bald white crown of rock completely bare of plant life, about the size of the suburb's old schoolyard. Gusts of wind swept across it, and Martin was nervous about standing up there, but Hertz evidently loved it.

"Look at that view!" he said.

Martin could see for miles back the way they had come. He saw part of the lake where Hertz had caught his fish, its canyon walls folding it into the surrounding landscape. Ahead lay the bright green land he'd seen earlier, big rectangles edged with pale beige, like a giant's tile floor. Not far from it were more regular spaces: square patches that were all one color, dark objects dotted at intervals along the hills, dark ribbons and lines crawling across them. Whatever these things were, Martin could tell one thing about them: they didn't belong to a natural landscape.

He walked over to Hertz, who was gazing at the sky and the pale, sculpted hills. "What is all that stuff?" he asked, pointing at the squares.

"Awful things," Hertz answered shortly. "I never go that way if I can help it. It's time," he went on, squinting at the sun. "Let's find out about your sister."

Hertz sat them both down near the center of their rocky stage and directed Martin to close his eyes. "Think of your question," he instructed. "Free your worries. Be receptive. The guidance comes from within you and all around."

It wasn't that Martin didn't try. He certainly would have liked to free his worries. But he kept peeking, and that probably didn't help. His companion sat cross-legged in a state of deep concentration, and Martin kept checking to see whether he had moved. The longer Hertz stayed relaxed, the more active Martin became. By the time Hertz opened his eyes, Martin was shifting from place to place as if he were sitting in nettles.

"Well?" asked Hertz. "Do you know where your sister is now? No? That's odd. Oh well, maybe tomorrow morning."

They clambered off the knob and headed toward their camping place. Martin was feeling puzzled. "Did you get any answers up there?" he asked.

"I sure did," said Hertz. "I learned that I should help you find your sister. It's very important. It may even be the reason I was put here on this Earth."

Martin felt even more bewildered and a little uncomfortable. He liked Hertz, but he wasn't sure he wanted such a devoted traveling companion, especially one with such strange intuitions. For the first time in hours, he glanced back at his dog. Chip was watching him like a prisoner being led away to die.

"Hertz, did the person who was important to you teach you about all that stuff?" he asked. "You know, going up on a hilltop to get answers?"

"What person?" asked Hertz with a slight frown.

"You know, the one from your past. The one you miss so much."

"I don't know what you're talking about," Hertz said. "I live alone. You're the first person I've ever met."

Martin was dumbfounded. But before he could argue, Hertz stopped them both with a gesture, pulling his knife from a loop on his knapsack. He silently shifted it to the other hand and then hurled it into the weeds ahead. There was a squeal and thrashing, and Hertz strode forward to collect his prize. "See?" He held up a bloodstained jackrabbit. "I never miss, Martin. Wait till you taste this!"

The evening was as awful as the day had been wonderful. For a couple of minutes, the dead rabbit looked like Cassie's plush toy. Then Hertz showed Martin how to skin it. He cooked it up and watched fondly as Martin choked it down, but he didn't eat any himself. "I told you I'm not hungry," he said. "Life out here takes discipline. You can't just do anything you want. Which reminds me. You need to learn the proper way to use the local water."

Crouching by a stream, he demonstrated the use of a water-filtering pump, filling one of Martin's empty water bottles. Then he broke the seal on a little medicine bottle and explained how it killed germs that lived in the water. Martin and Chip watched solemnly, as if they expected an exam to follow. Now, everywhere that Hertz went, two apprehensive pairs of eyes studied his every move.

When night fell, the big man took a foil pouch out of his knapsack and ripped it open. "Wrap yourself up in this," he directed. "You'll stay warmer."

Martin received the thin metallic sheet without protest or comment and did as he was told. He stayed warm too: that night, he was as comfortable as he had ever been outside a suburb. But his dreams were garish. Shiny bright skillets and plastic-handled forks danced around and taunted him. Sharp buck knives climbed out of knapsacks and hunted him down.

A poke on the shoulder roused him from sleep, and those pale blue eyes were the first thing he saw. No wonder he let out a yell.

"Hey, nothing's wrong," said Hertz. "I'm going to climb my hill again. Want to come? It's a great way to start off the day."

Martin sat up and shook his head. "No thanks," he muttered. "I'd just slow you down."

"Okay then. Back in a bit. I'll keep an eye on you, don't worry."

Martin watched Hertz dwindle into the distance, then come back into view as he began his climb into the cloudy sky. Sure enough, Hertz was keeping an eye on him. The minuscule figure waved cheerfully in his direction from time to time. Hertz didn't spend many minutes on the morning ritual either. It wasn't long before he was coming back down.

Chip crept over and laid his furry head in Martin's lap. Although Martin breathed easier knowing that their strange companion was away, the shepherd seemed just as frightened as if Hertz were there. Those dark eyes pleaded with Martin for understanding.

"I dreamt about camping supplies," Martin told him. "All night long. Bright shiny skillets and bright plastic-handled forks, without a single scratch. Without . . . a single scratch."

Suddenly, the air seemed frigid. He felt the blood drain from his face. "And bottles that have never been opened," he whispered. "And blankets that were never used. Chip! His clothes are so old that they're falling off, but his camping gear's never been touched!"

Chip licked Martin's hand, as if to signal his approval.

"This is wrong," Martin breathed. "This is bad. Very, very bad. We can't run. He'll find us. Can't hide. I can't fight him. And I don't know what's going on. Chip, I know you do. I know he did something—threatened you, threatened me, maybe—but you have to help me figure this out."

The dog's intelligent brown eyes gazed up at him, and he thought Chip was about to give him a sign. But at that moment, they heard a halloo from across the field. The shepherd ducked away as if it were gunfire.

Now that he knew they were in serious trouble, Martin felt more composed. He mustn't rouse any suspicions, so he prepared himself to act normal. That shouldn't be too hard. All he had to do was keep behaving like a kid.

"Any new answers?" he asked as Hertz strode up.

"No," replied Hertz serenely. "But that's okay. It's just good to know we're not alone in this world."

They prepared to break camp. Crouching over his knapsack, Hertz packed up his pristine gear while Martin put on his sneakers and picked the burrs out of his rapidly fuzzing socks. Chip slunk up beside him and copied him, gnawing at a front paw as if he were trying to extract a sticker from between his pads.

"You silly dog," Martin told him in a low voice. "You never get stickers! They slide . . . right . . . off."

Slowly, he turned his head until Hertz came into view. The big man was still on his knees, checking over his gear. Old socks, but no stickers. No mud from last night's water pumping. No blood from the rabbit. Old clothes, but no new stains. No new stains at all.

Casually, Martin reached for his backpack. He felt around for an eternity, past Cassie's old bunny, past all those half-melted snack bars, until he found what he was looking for. Then, slowly, he walked over to Hertz and dropped his Alldog reset chip onto the man's shoulder.

They probably made a chip especially for bots like this one. In any case, this chip didn't work very well on him. Hertz didn't just become a neat pool of simulation gel. That would have been too easy.

Hertz shrieked and flung himself wildly about, reaching out in all directions. He seemed to sink into quicksand up to his waist: first his legs and then his hips were gone. He flung out his arms: two arms, then four, six, ten, twelve arms that writhed like fleshy snakes and grabbed for Martin. The agony on his face was beyond description.

Then he collapsed in on himself. His head caved in like an empty shell. For a time, the face still floated on the silver liquid, mouthing silent pleas or curses. At long last, it faded away into the shiny surface like a lost reflection.

Martin became aware that someone was shaking him. It was Chip, pressed against his legs, shivering so violently that they were both in danger of toppling. Martin knelt and wrapped his arms around the dog.

"That can't be fun to watch, can it?" he said. "It was bad enough for me, but it was more weird than anything. For you, it must be like watching your own murder."

Hertz was nothing more now than an oblong of silver gel. Floating inside was a big green circuit board, bristling with chips of all descriptions. But there were a couple of odd things floating in there too. One was a long, loose spring running from a closed metal box to what looked like an electrical plug. Two large copper prongs stuck out from the plug, each about an inch long.

"Hey, Chip, what's that?" Martin asked.

Chip spoke for the first time since Hertz's arrival. He lifted his muzzle and let out a tormented howl.

"It's a killer then," Martin guessed. "A weapon that kills bots as well as people. When Hertz came along, he must have showed it to you. He held up his hand so I couldn't see, and he told you to keep quiet. Because otherwise—well, of course!—you'd talk to him in bot, and then I would have known he was bad news."

But if the weapon had terrified Chip, it was the other discovery that chilled Martin. Coiled up in Hertz's gel was a radio antenna. This bot was wired for long-distance communication.

Don't you ever get the feeling that we're surrounded by forces we can't see? Twice a day, I go up high. And I seek guidance, and I find answers. It's good to know we're not alone in this world.

Martin stared at the antenna and felt like howling right along with Chip. Hertz was a unique and very powerful bot, loaded with features and brand-new supplies. He had been entrusted with an extremely important mission, the reason for his whole existence. And that mission was keeping an eye on Martin Glass.

CHAPTER TWELVE

They escaped as quickly as they could. Martin took the mustard-colored knapsack, loading the snack bars and his flashlight on top of the camping equipment and tying Cassie's bunny to a strap. It was heavier than his backpack, but the supplies were so valuable that he couldn't risk leaving them behind.

"Why do they care what I'm up to?" he demanded as they walked away. "Why me? I'm just one little kid from the burb. If they catch me, it's game shows for sure." He quaked at the thought.

The day promised to stay cool. Fluffy gray clouds blanketed the sky from one horizon to the other as they walked up the packet line toward the artificial landscape he had seen the evening before. A few hours into their walk, Martin saw to his dismay that the packet line split again, going three ways this time. One line continued straight, one line headed left toward the nearby mountains, and one line headed east, along the very edge of that green land that had looked like a giant's floor.

"Fantastic!" he wailed. "Three ways this time, and not a clue which way that Motley guy went!"

They came to the rails that ran to the east, cutting across their line of march. Martin scrambled up the steep gravel bank, and the mystery of the bright green zone revealed itself. The tiles were large cultivated fields, containing row after row of identical plants. Silver bots worked there, moving between the rows.

"I see food, Chip! Let's go get some."

They clambered down the gravel bank and crossed the weedy stretch of ground before the first field. Martin slowed down as they approached. "That's kind of funny," he said.

Up to the edge of the field were wildflowers and weeds, but the tidy field held nothing but one kind of plant. Outside it, bees and flies hummed, grasshoppers hopped, and beetles and butterflies spread their wings. Inside, not so much as a single ant moved along the bare earth. Martin could see no barrier around the field, but everything unwanted stayed outside.

"Chip, do you see a fence?" he asked.

As if sharing his thoughts, a bee flew toward the field. When it reached the edge, a small space before it darkened as if it cast a shadow in the air, and it bounced into an invisible barrier with a small thump. Over and over, it thumped itself against this blockade. Then it flew off in a less discouraging direction.

Martin tapped at the air with a cautious finger. Sure enough, as low or as high as he could reach, his fingernail hit something hard, like glass.

"That's just great!" he said. "We're not going this way. And those are ripe tomatoes too!"

Beside him, Chip studied the rustling rows of plants and their attendant agricultural bots. In a few seconds, a small silver bot temporarily augmented their workforce. It plucked several tomatoes and rolled back out again. Then it transformed back into a German shepherd and danced with pleasure at the successful completion of its mission.

"You know, you like being a dog, don't you?" Martin observed, biting into one of the tomatoes. "I mean, you'll change and everything, but you never want to *stay* changed."

For answer, Chip crouched down in a playful feint, poked Martin with a tan paw, and wagged his bushy black tail.

They walked along the edge of the fields for hours, trying out different kinds of produce along the way. At first, Martin hung back when the agricultural bots were working nearby, but they paid no attention to him. He caught several glimpses of a strange spectacle ahead, but for quite a while, they walked past high rows of corn and could see nothing of it at all. Then they climbed the crest of a mounded bank, and the view unfolded itself, stark and clear, against the cloudy sky.

"What's *that*?" Martin wondered, shading his eyes.

It was an immense, airy sculpture, a three-dimensional diagram of a shoelace knot, sprawled over a region as large as his entire suburb. Great ribbons of concrete rose gracefully into the air and doubled over one another in long curves. Martin could trace them as they climbed from one side and crossed to the other in long ramps and huge circles: sidestepping, diverging, and merging again, like a ballet of motion stopped and frozen forever. One above another, the thin stone ribbons rose into the air, until the one at the top was five layers high. Martin stared at its dizzying height in rapture.

"I have *got* to get up there!"

This was easier said than done. He could track the soaring span to its earthly origin, but that was still far away. Once he got closer, he found that the massive artwork was protected by steep banks and dense scrub. But he reached the source at last: a broken-up bed of dark gray asphalt, choked with bushes and weeds. Only when the structure left the ground did the weeds stay behind and the pitted surface become sturdy concrete.

"This is a street," he said as they walked up it. "All of these things look like streets. Streets in the air, running all over the place! How weird is that?"

The climb was strenuous. Martin was glad that the overcast day was cool because he was soon panting with fatigue. He walked up the middle of the worn roadbed, staying away from the low concrete barriers at the edges. Suburbs were flat. Aside from his climb with Hertz, he had never been anywhere high.

The top of the span would have pleased Hertz, but Martin felt uneasy at the thought of how far up he was and how little solid support there seemed to be around him. Even the road itself wasn't flat. It angled in an alarming way, with a high side and a low side. He crawled to the high side to look over.

Directly below, like a big dark gash, stretched the remnants of a majestic road. Trees grew out of it now, but it had been very wide, and he could follow it with his eyes a long way into the distance. The packet line crossed it on a low, flat bridge, just as if it were a river. Another roadway, almost as wide, came up to meet this one. It was their junction that created the enormous knot of roads and ramps. Martin was consumed with admiration at the planning of it all.

"I think it's beautiful!" he told Chip. "Why'd they let it fall apart?"

He followed the packet line with his eyes, trying to gauge how likely it was as a route for the Wonder Baby packet. It ran toward a confusing clutter of artificial-looking elements in the distance: tall structures, gathered together in a ruinous tumble, like the stack of firewood Hertz had lit to cook his rabbit. Martin squinted at them but could make out little about them beyond their height and lack of uniformity. Light glinted back at him from some areas, as if some parts were glass, but other parts were as black as holes. All in all, they formed a bizarre collage on the far horizon that signified to him neither pattern nor meaning.

Martin was more interested in the land that lay almost directly below him, right on the other side of the ruined road crossed by the packet line. This region was close enough to see clearly, so he could understand more things about it. It was mostly forest, full of native vegetation, so its color was close to the olive green of the hills that he had traveled. But it was woven through with what had plainly been at one time a net of closely drawn streets, and many dark structures still lined the roadways. The buildings' outlines were ragged and damaged with age and encroaching brush, but they were regular, like a baby's blocks.

Martin gazed down at the spiderweb of streets and the boxes that lined them. The scene tugged at him, as if he should recognize it somehow. Cool wind poured past him, and he looked around. The clouds were growing thicker.

"Come on, Chip," he said. "Let's keep going that way. I want to see what's down there in those little streets."

They were easier to study from above than on the ground. Swallowed up by trees and enormous bushes, they were in a tangle of foliage so thick that Martin couldn't force his way through. Then Chip found a wreck of broken paving that turned toward the area, probably one of those little streets Martin had seen from the air. The crumbling surface at least discouraged the exuberant plant growth, even if it couldn't stop it.

Martin walked along the street, looking about. The forest of scrubby oaks and diseased sycamores and ashes turned the street into an airy tunnel, and matted leaves and plant roots tripped him whenever he was unwise enough to take too many steps without looking down. The dark structures were man-made buildings, just as he had thought, spaced about ten feet apart from one another on both sides of the road. Enormous, ragged bushes growing up before them blocked most of his view, and yet they seemed eerily familiar.

Here, where the plant growth was sparse in front of the buildings, large concrete slabs came down to join the street, their surfaces shattered like jigsaw puzzles. He had never seen anything like them. Of course not. How could he have? And yet, the regularity of them, as he walked along, spoke like a whisper in his mind: curb, space, curb, space. He stopped to calm the disquieting feeling, studying a busted slab, looking at the crumbled curbing beside it, its chunks like a dropped and broken piecrust. But the minute he started walking, the feeling started up again.

A chilly wind came winding down through the lemon-and-lime-colored forest, shaking the dried weeds at his feet. But those—were *they* weeds? Those showy dark red flowers, whipping back and forth on that straggling vine? Surely those hadn't grown there by themselves. Surely he had seen them before.

Yard work isn't for everybody, but I take pride in it. It wouldn't kill some people to do a little work around here.

"Oh no," he whispered.

Stillness blanketed the empty neighborhood. Against the low black clouds, the shabby leaves seemed bright. Martin felt a sickness falling into the pit of his stomach, an aching dread that came from not wanting to learn what he already knew.

Pale pink brick on a tumbledown structure, light brown brick on the next, matching one another in form and feature across a riot of tangled growth. Picture window, front door, gap for a garage door; picture window, front door, garage. The patterns of things were revealing themselves, pushing their way through the branches and leaf mold: the spaces and rhythms that governed a way of life.

They found a building less damaged than the others and entered through the garage—of course, his heart told him as he gathered courage in the semidarkness, because he always entered through the garage. He pushed his way through the remains of the door, and there they were, just as he had known they would be: the kitchen, the dining room, the living room over there, where the breeze curled through what had been the picture window. In the murky gloom, those familiar places seemed to gather around him, as if they had been waiting for his arrival to give them their form.

"I don't believe this!" said Martin shakily. "Chip, we're home."

He stepped over drifted leaves and peered through the darkness at shelves that still held plates, at cabinets that had warped and disgorged their contents—cans and broken bottles—onto the uneven counters and floor. He gingerly pulled a brittle syrup container from the filth and held it up. The one he used every Rest Day was this same shape.

Nudging past the upended structure that had once stood on four legs and been the dining table, he made his way toward the living room. Things that might have once been chairs snapped and crunched under his feet, but the kitchen bar was still intact. As he passed it, he seemed to see, out of the corner of his eye, the shadow of a woman bending over a coffee cup.

Where had this woman gone? And why?

Now he stood in the living room and looked out through the picture window at the bushes that were growing in. Had that misshapen lump that sprouted weeds along its length once been a family couch? Could that black hulk by the wall be the shell of a television? What had they watched in the evening, this missing family? And why—*why*—were they gone?

Our families were the lucky ones. He had heard that so many times. But what had happened to the ones who hadn't been lucky?

Our grandparents competed for the right to live in comfort. Yes, but people were supposed to be dying then. Sickness and poverty, wasn't that right? But this looked like a fine place to live.

Suppose, when they had built the domed suburbs in Granny's day—tiny copies of this huge one, obviously—suppose that this suburb had still been alive and well. They couldn't have moved everybody into the domes. There would have been far too many people. Somehow, they had chosen who would survive. There had to have been some kind of lottery, some sort of competition.

Or maybe . . . maybe even a game show.

An appalling idea! An idea so ghastly, Martin couldn't even bring himself to say it out loud. *We are not going to discuss this. Sometimes it's best to turn your back on things.* For how many generations now had his people been turning their backs on things? How long had they sat in their living rooms and watched other people die?

A strong gust of wind blasted into the deserted room, and Martin beat a hasty retreat. Outside and overhead, rattling drops hit the roof as he stumbled down the murky hall. The first room he came to had a nice window through which he could see the whipping trees. Martin was glad to emerge from the darkness. He was afraid of the darkness in his thoughts.

The small space was full of junk and debris, and spiders and insects fled at his intrusion. He picked up a plastic puzzle cube, stripped of its colors but just like the one he had at home. This room, a prickling intuition suggested, had belonged to a boy his own age.

And in a flash, he felt that boy standing right behind him.

He dropped the cube and whirled, knowing that nothing would be there. Nothing was. But the air was palpable with loathing and bitterness.

Don't you ever get the feeling that we're surrounded by forces we can't see? Forces that hate us for the things we did to them.

Martin spent the storm huddled in the dim hallway, with his arms wrapped tightly around Chip. Water poured through cracks in the ceiling and soaked him to the skin. Thunder crashed, and lightning flashed red against his eyelids, but the violence of the weather was no less terrifying than the violence in his own mind. It isn't my fault that we won and you lost, he pleaded with the house's silent spirits. He didn't dare to look up for fear of the faces he might see.

Long before the last rumbles of thunder faded, Martin scurried from the house, his anxious dog trotting at his heels. He bolted down the center of the weedy, muddy street, not daring now to look left or right. He could feel stern gazes from those gaping picture windows, the implacable resentment of the dead. *What right has one of the lucky ones to come here,* they seemed to ask, *when we were the ones who paid the price?*

Chip led him out of the tangle of overgrown streets and back to the mammoth knot of ramps and bridges. Martin picked out the most direct bridge to the green produce fields and dashed across it as if they were followed by an army of ghosts. On the other side of the wide gash that had been the great roadway, he collapsed in relief and looked back at the low growth of forest that hid its dismal secret so well.

"It's like this, Chip," he said, taking a long drink of water. "I can't believe Motley went this way. Everything this way is dead." He shuddered. "Worse than dead! So no one brought a packet car down this line. We'll follow the line that goes the other way."

They retraced their route as quickly as possible, coming to the junction in the packet lines before nightfall. Here, Martin led them west, toward the mountains that had long fascinated him. He had no good reason to make that choice over going to the north, as they had been doing. Probably, he just wanted to put as much distance as possible between himself and the decomposed suburb.

All of Hertz's camping gear couldn't make Martin comfortable that night. Over and over, Chip woke him out of terrifying dreams. As the night wore on, even the bot seemed to be losing composure, whimpering as he watched his master fight a battle he couldn't understand. "You're lucky you don't dream, Chip," Martin told him.

The crags that began the mountain range were close now, but at first, the route toward them only served to depress Martin further. This was the trash line, and the colored squares he had seen from Hertz's high knob of ground were dumps of all descriptions, one right after another, with a short packet line running to each. Here was a huge appliance dump, with crushed metal cubes rusting in geometric heaps. Next came a plastic dump, its colors bleaching away in the bright sunshine.

The strangest of all was a shoe dump, a hole the size of a city block full of old shoes, baking in the warm morning with a heady aroma. Martin stared at it in wonder.

"My old Hermies are in there somewhere," he mourned. "I swear, it's all I can do to keep from diving in to look for them. Mom threw them out last summer, right before school started. Nothing's felt that good on my feet since."

By midday, the first steep hills of the mountain range were upon them, and the packet line began to curve and wind to find its path. Then they came to the ultimate trash dump, a place to dispose of the packet cars themselves. The deserted rail yard was old and vast, spread across a flat stretch of ground caught between the foothills and the nearest of the tall granite crags. Many rusting lines fanned out across it to hold hundreds, if not thousands, of unused packets. Nothing moved in that enormous parking lot. It was truly the end of the line.

"This is just perfect!" Martin said. "After all that walking, we have to go back again and take the other line. I don't guess any-one ever comes this way."

But Chip trotted ahead, looking interested. He picked out one of the many packet lines that crossed the dusty yard and followed it.

"What's up?" Martin asked. "I don't see the point." Then, after a minute, he thought he did. The other rails were dull, but sunlight gleamed off the set of rails they were following. This packet line had recently been used.

The line led them in a wide arc around to the far corner of the yard. Here, long, low, open-sided sheds protected a select set of cars. The rails ran under the shadow of one of their tin roofs and ended at a tarpaulin-swathed packet. Martin loosened a corner of the gray tarp and peeked underneath. The packet car was bright red.

"Chip, you're a genius! It's Motley's car!"

Further investigation confirmed his hunch. There couldn't be two cars like this. But it was abandoned.

"Where did he take them?" Martin wondered as they stood in the shade beside the car. "There aren't any kids here. This place is way too quiet. Do you have any more hunches?" Chip laid back his velvet ears and wagged regretfully. "Okay then. We have to think this through."

Martin sat down on the packet platform and fortified himself with his last piece of bubble gum, chewing thoughtfully until he had it broken in.

"So Motley uses this packet to carry the Exponents. Let's say he gets them where he wants them. Then he's got to get rid of the car so none of us can find it and find him. He ditches the car here, where it mixes in with all the other packets. But he's not here. So he does one of two things. He either swipes another packet or he walks home. But this is the only line that's been used, so Motley walked wherever he was going."

He backed up and peered over the top of the tin roof to get his bearings. Steep slopes dotted with short bushes hemmed in the yard on this side, breaking now and then into sheer rock faces that would support no vegetation. Behind them, he saw even steeper slopes and higher crags. The mountain range began here in earnest.

"Unless he flew," he amended. "Maybe you could walk up there, Chip, but I don't think I could, and I don't think Cassie could, either. But he didn't take the kids back the way we came because there was nothing back there but dumps. Maybe they went somewhere on scooters. Let's check for tracks."

This turned out to be a waste of time. The storm that had drenched them yesterday had washed away any traces there might have been. And it occurred to Martin that Motley could have dropped off the children before coming here to leave the packet. Finding the car didn't prove anything after all. Cassie still might be far away.

A sharp bark interrupted this gloomy train of thought, and Martin went to investigate. At the very back of the yard, under the shadow of a granite cliff, the long tin awnings ended in a series of small cinder-block sheds, each about ten feet square. Chip stood in front of one shed, wagging furiously.

"Chip, these are just little storage rooms, like a garage," Martin said. "I bet they're full of packet junk, like Dad's storage rooms near the loading bay." But Chip just became more excited. He bounded up and put his tan feet against Martin's chest.

"Okay then, show me. Make this good."

The door was locked, but not for long, and the enthusiastic dog soon pulled down the shelves that stood behind it. A steel door was fitted into the back of the shed and, beyond it, a dark passageway.

"Whoa!" Martin said. "That can't be here! These things are

little squares." He stepped out of the shed and looked around. "No, I get it—the rest are right next to the cliff, but this one backs up against it. You'd never know it, though. It looks like it's just an accident, to keep them all in a nice even line."

They entered the tunnel. Chip trotted along first, eyes aglow, and Martin followed him. The passageway was dark, winding, and creepy, but comfortable and clean. It was just wide and high enough that Martin didn't need to stoop and his knapsack didn't get caught on the walls. It had chiseled sides and a concrete floor. Long flights of steps interrupted its progress from time to time.

For an eternity, they trooped along through the solid rock of the mountain, stopping to rest now and then. The passage turned and curved, ascended and descended, but never branched or split. "Good thing," said Martin. "If we came to another passage, we wouldn't have a clue which way to go. I just wish I knew how much longer this is gonna go on. I'm starting to get creeped out."

At last, a glimmer appeared ahead. Martin thought it was just his imagination until they came around a sharp curve and almost fell into the daylight.

They stepped out onto an outcrop of gray rock that over-looked a little valley full of fir trees. The mountains enfolded this shadowed hollow in tall, stony splendor. Martin had to tilt his head far back to see past their craggy walls to a small circle of pale blue sky.

"You know, Chip, this is really pretty," he said.

"TRESPASSERS WILL BE ELECTROCUTED," a voice roared in answer, and Chip fell motionless at Martin's feet.

CHAPTER THIRTEEN

A massive bot stepped out of the tunnel behind Martin. Twice as large and half again as tall as the biggest man Martin had ever seen, the apparition was clad from head to toe in silver-gray body armor. It didn't seem to belong in that idyllic mountain setting. It would have been more at home in the dimly lit underworld of HM1 or perhaps in Martin's nightmares. Its face was a blank mask of disinterested menace.

"TRESPASSERS WILL BE ELECTROCUTED," it blared again in a resonating rumble, like a roomful of double bassoons. "YOUR BOT HAS CLEARLY TRESPASSED."

"My dog!" wailed Martin and dropped to his knees on the uneven stone. Chip lay on his side, eyes staring, mouth open, and legs flung out as stiffly as an overturned chair. Martin tried to smooth his rough fur and cried out in pain. His hand felt as if it had been jabbed with sewing needles.

"PLEASE EXERCISE CAUTION," advised the enormous battle bot, a note of worry creeping in among the bassoons. "FROZEN SIMULATION GEL CAN BE HAZARDOUS TO THE TOUCH."

"You killed my dog!" Martin cried, weeping furiously. "You stupid jerk! You stupid, stupid moron!"

The steely bot crouched beside Chip, and Martin shrank away, wiping a forearm across his wet cheeks. Had he just imagined the thing's size before? It was big, yes, but not enormous.

"I DID NOT KILL THIS BOT," it informed him civilly, the bassoons now playing pianissimo. "ITS SUBROUTINES ARE

INTERRUPTED. IT NEEDS TO BE RESET." It reached out a gray arm to touch the dog, and Martin wiped his eyes again. Arm—or armor? He was getting confused. He kept seeing things.

Chip melted with a whisper into silver gelatin, and Martin waited for the ovoid pool to reform. After a minute, he realized that nothing was happening.

"Hey!" he protested. He tried to recapture the anger he had felt before, but it eluded him now. He just felt tearful and wretched—and frightened. The big bot watched him from behind the blankness of its armor. Martin had a fleeting impression of a wrinkled face superimposed upon that shiny mask, as if, for just a second or two, an old man had used it for a mirror.

"I discharged your bot's batteries," the bot explained, its sound reduced to a half dozen tubas. *"This bot must remain nonfunctioning until my orders change. It is a trespasser. My orders are very clear about trespassers. About you, my orders are not so clear."*

Martin peered at the bot. Yes, it definitely had a face. Blue eyes were peering back at him through the clear shell of the mask, blue eyes under thick white eyebrows.

"Well, what are your orders?" Martin asked hoarsely.

"Trespassers will be ELECTROCUTED." A blast of bassoon underscored this familiar phrase. *"Are you a trespasser?"* the bot went on. *"It's a simple question; you ought to know."*

Martin licked his lips and poked Chip's simulation gel, which was something he had always wanted to do. The gel felt springy and hard, like rubber.

"You know," he pointed out, "we humans don't electrocute so good. I mean, you zap us and poof! That's the ball game. No resets with us."

To his surprise, the battle bot nodded. It had acquired a distinct impression of age. It now stooped over the puddled Chip, no larger than Martin's own father. "I'm aware of that," it said in a voice like a rather cautious oboe. "That's why I want to be sure. I'd hate to make a mistake."

Martin pondered the machine's alterations. He wasn't losing his mind, he decided. It seemed to be losing its mind. Simple programming, he reminded himself. That's the secret to bots.

"Well," he asked, "if you don't think I'm a trespasser, then what do you think I am?"

The bot was silent for several seconds as it puzzled over the question. Its features, vague and indistinct, flickered like a bad hologram. "I think . . . ," it admitted finally, "I really think . . . that you might be a child." As Martin stared in amazement, a kindly face supplanted the battle mask. It had white hair and a long flowing beard. "And if you're a child," it continued, "then I have to get you to school. Electrocution would never do, you see."

A gentle old man knelt on the rock now in soft, steely gray robes. He was gazing at Martin with mild blue eyes.

"Oh, I am *definitely* a child," Martin said. "You better get me to school right away."

"Wonderful!" cried the old man. "I was sure of it! It's a very good thing I was careful. Rudy would have been cross with me for days if I had electrocuted a student." He rose to his sandaled feet and flopped the thick silver pancake that was Chip over his shoulder. "We'll take your friend along too. I'd better bring you to William first; yes, William's in charge right now."

They climbed down the granite outcrop and crossed the little valley under the shade of the fir trees. Martin had to trot to keep up with the bent old bot. "You're a student I don't believe I've met before," he noted. "Martin, is it? Delighted to meet you. They call me Sim."

Some distance from the outcrop, well under the shadow of the sheltering mountains, they came around a bend in the rock and entered a shallow cave. It wasn't a cave for long. Sim pushed open a pair of industrial-looking metal doors and led Martin down a passage very much like the factory corridors or the halls off the loading bay. Offices, rooms, and other hallways split off on one side or the other.

"Wow!" Martin said. "I never would have known all this was here."

"Certainly not," Sim agreed, hobbling along beside him. "What's the point of making a secret government facility if everyone can tell it's there? This one is so secret that not even the government seems to know about it anymore; at least, that's what Rudy hopes."

He knocked at a door, and a muffled voice summoned them. He cast a worried glance at Martin. "I do hope you don't get into trouble."

They entered a small office piled high with computer equipment and mounds of white sheets of paper. These items perched on or fell off the central piece of furniture, a very large ugly metal desk. The desk seemed to be not so much a place to put down the handhelds and papers as a magnet to attract them in drifts. This left very little room to walk, so Martin stopped right inside the door.

Two plain wooden chairs stood in the room. One, propped invitingly near the door, could have held Martin if it weren't already holding two reams of paper in a big cardboard box. The other, behind the desk, was already occupied. It held the most beautiful girl he had ever seen.

The girl came around the desk to meet them. She was about Martin's age, but while he had been growing straight up, all her growth had gone to soft curves. Her thick hair was brown, with warm highlights, and her eyes were large and green. Just at the moment, those green eyes weren't very friendly.

"Sim, what is this?" she demanded.

"Martin is a new student," Sim said. "He and his companion bot came to the school just now. I followed them through the passage and made sure they were alone. He cried when I disrupted his bot, so I realized he had to be a child."

Martin squirmed a little over this report. "You didn't have to tell her that!" he said. Then he remembered how quickly this bot could cease to be a gentle old man.

"A new student," the girl said dubiously. "Martin just hiked in to our mountain retreat and decided to enroll."

"Indeed, yes," Sim assured her, with an encouraging nod to Martin. "He wanted me to take him to class right away, didn't you?"

"Well, yeah," Martin replied as innocently as possible. "I'm a typical kid. I like school."

This statement only seemed to annoy the girl. "You *hate* school," she informed him. "Let's dispense with the absurdities. Your model makes an unpersuasive liar. Tell me who sent you here and how many of you know about this place."

"Oh my," sighed the friendly old bot. "I was afraid you'd get into trouble." He slung Chip's oblong gel from his shoulder and set it down with a wobbly *boing*. "Better be ready," he explained mournfully, "in case I have to electrocute you."

"Hey, look, nobody sent me," Martin said. "I ran away. Nobody knows about your mountain re-re—I mean, school. We even locked the door behind us." Only after saying this did he realize he might have been unwise. If they were looking to solve their problems by eliminating him, he had played right into their hands. "But hey—you should know that my friends are gonna be really upset if you electrocute me. I mean, I don't think you want that kind of trouble."

"Martin has a good point," Sim said, eager to put in a good word. "It would probably make his friends cry too."

The girl listened attentively. Her green eyes gave no sign that his arguments were working. Martin noticed she had a dusting of freckles across her nose. He thought they were cute, and that thought immediately struck him as pathetic.

"Sim, bring him along," the girl directed and led them out of the office.

Martin followed her down the sterile hallway, feeling angry with himself. Chip was gone, and he had acted like a brainless, whiny idiot in front of a girl his own age. He wished he could have returned her indifferent stare with one of his own, but Sim would have had to electrocute him first. It wasn't her clothing, which was simple enough: she had belted a knee-length blue T-shirt to wear it as a dress, and her red high-top sneakers looked comfortably broken in. But somehow, on her, the plain T-shirt and high-tops seemed gorgeously feminine, as if she were wearing one of baby Laura's party dresses. And her brown hair twinkled, he noticed, every time they walked under a bank of lights. Not fair! Martin protested to the universe at large. This is *not* fair!

"Leave your pack here in the hall," she commanded, and then led the way into a large white-tiled shower room. "First things first," she said, setting supplies on a three-legged chair by one of the dripping stalls. "Sim, our intruder needs a bath."

"Well, duh!" Martin said bitterly. "I was running for my life through weeds and dumps. I didn't exactly have a bathroom following me around." She left without bothering to answer.

Oh, but that shower was wonderful! Martin scrubbed and scrubbed, and soaped, and rinsed, and scrubbed and scrubbed again. When he emerged, Sim gave him new clothes. The bot mopped up water and cleaned twigs and grass out of the shower stall while Martin got dressed.

It felt good to put on clean stuff, he decided generously, even if it wasn't his. A loose blue T-shirt, jeans that were not quite long enough, white socks that were thicker than he really cared for—

"Hey! Where's my sneakers?" he demanded. "These aren't mine."

Sim didn't leave off his cleaning. "For questions about your clothes, you need to see William," he replied. "I'm just a bot. William's in charge."

"Well, let's do it, then!"

Sim conducted him through the maze of hallways to a small, bright, bare meeting room furnished with a cheap dinette set of imitation wood. The room would have felt crowded and claustrophobic except for the large mirror that took up most of the back wall. It gave an illusion of greater space.

The brown-haired girl sat on top of the table, her red high-tops resting on the seat of a chair. She was busy typing into a large handheld that rested on her lap. She looked up at their entrance and saw the shoes in Martin's hands. The corner of her mouth twitched.

"Is something the matter?"

"These things aren't mine!" Martin brandished the sneakers.

"No. They're new. Yours were falling apart."

"They were not! They were perfectly good—"

"Cracked and dirty—"

"Just the way I like them, and I *demand* to know what you did with my—"

"Gone."

"Gone?" Martin stared at her, dumbfounded. "*Gone?!* You dumped my *shoes?*"

At the look on his face, the girl burst out laughing. Then she hopped off the table and retrieved his old sneakers from a cardboard box in the corner.

"Sorry about that," she said. "A behavioral experiment. I wanted to know if all Fourteens were irrationally devoted to their worn-out clothing. And—" She couldn't even finish the sentence. She just waved her hands toward his shoes.

Martin glowered as he put them on. "They're perfectly *fine*," he muttered. This would have sent her off into fresh gales of laughter if she weren't already laughing as hard as she could.

"I had them fumigated," she announced brightly as soon as she was able to speak.

To the end of his days, Martin's brain would collect devastating replies to this insult, but unfortunately, it didn't start right away.

He had to lace his sneakers in humiliating silence.

"Look, can we just go see this William guy now?" he said when he was done. "I'm ready to talk to somebody in charge."

The girl's laughter switched off with the abruptness of a packet car wreck. She sat down on the table and crossed her arms. "You're talking to her," she said coldly. "I *am* William."

Martin felt his ears heat up.

"It doesn't matter," she went on. "I need to go to class. Rudy already knows you're here, so he's coming in a minute. In the meantime, Sim is standing guard outside the door. I don't think he'll go through with the electrocution order because he seems rather protective of you, but he's certainly going to keep you from leaving." She tossed her handheld into the cardboard box, picked up the box, and departed.

Martin prowled the small room after her exit, feeling ill at ease. Aside from having cleaned up and changed clothes, he hadn't gained much since his arrival. He knew nothing about who was holding him, he'd lost track of Chip, and he had bolted out of the shower room so quickly that he had forgotten his knapsack.

He poked his head out the door. The aged bot was loitering in the hallway outside. "Sim!" he called. "I need my dog. Can I go get him?"

"Your bot is still charging," Sim said. "Its batteries were low. What did you need?"

"Well . . . nothing, I guess. Can I get my gear, then?"

"Your pack? I'm afraid not," said the old man. "Some of the items were dangerous. Rudy has to decide about you before you can have it back."

"Okay." Martin shut the door again. There was no way around it. They had him trapped. Interesting how the ones who could kill him always seemed like the nicest people.

Then he remembered something odd. That girl William had called him a Fourteen. But she wasn't the first person to do so. Someone else had called him that too.

You were the very best model of your year. Not so good at talking, though. When it comes to that, Fourteens are easy to outsmart.

The door opened, and Motley walked in.

CHAPTER FOURTEEN

The young man no longer wore bright, splashy colors. He was dressed exactly like Martin, in a blue T-shirt and jeans. But this didn't dim his remarkable appearance in the least. Like the lovely William, he was a star.

"You!" cried Martin, stunned.

"You!" said Motley, looking pleased to see him. "When I got word that a Dish Fourteen was in our facility, I immediately thought of you. You and that fancy bot of yours. If every Fourteen had a modified bot, this would be a different world."

Martin refused to fall for his charm. "What have you done with her?" he demanded furiously. "Where's Cassie? And none of your tricks!"

"Cassie," pondered the young man. "Cassie is in geometry at the moment; I believe they're taking an exam. I'll call her out so you can visit with her as soon as we've finished our talk." When Martin stared at him wildly, he sat down on one of the chairs and spread his hands in a mollifying gesture. "I told you when I came that I was taking her to a special school. That's exactly what I did."

So it had all been perfectly fine! Cassie had just gone to school. This man had come, the parents had voted, and the children had been thrilled to go.

"No," Martin said, and he shook his head violently. His hands were beginning to tremble. "You weren't there to take them to a school. You were there for the product recall. My dad didn't believe in that special school for a minute."

"Let me get this straight," Motley said, leaning forward. "You didn't believe that I told the truth because the packet chief thought I was lying. But he only cooperated with me in the first place because he thought I was lying. Our whole society is based on lies, on the myth of the blowing sand and poison gas. So you think I made the truth into one of my tricks."

"Well—yes," Martin stammered. "At least, I think that's what I think."

"You're right, I did," Motley agreed.

"Stop it!" Martin cried. "I'm tired of you doing that!"

"What, talk circles around you?" Motley smiled. "Fair enough, Fourteen. I'll try to stop."

"And Cassie's really safe with you?" Martin asked. Motley nodded. "And nothing bad happened to her? No recall?" Motley shook his head.

"Well, then I just don't get it," Martin said dolefully. "I mean, not at all. About the suburbs. The sand. The whole big neighborhood out there that's empty and falling down. Why all the lies? I mean, *why*? None of it makes any sense!"

Motley folded his arms and leaned back in his chair. "It was all done with you in mind," he said. "Close to a hundred years ago, our nation was slowly decaying. Handhelds and robots had just been invented, and that meant factories didn't need so many humans to work in them anymore. The armies didn't need them either, because war was changing too. Killing people wasn't important. It was which factories and machines you could blow up, and the robots were getting better at doing that than the humans were. All these unneeded people were crowding up the cities—suburbs, you'd call them—eating food and getting sick and demanding medicine. They cost more to keep than they could earn, and they were fouling up the air and water, too. New people were being born every day."

"Born?" Martin asked.

"The stork kept bringing them."

"Oh, I get it. And then what?"

"Then a certain President came along. A real man of vision. And he knew just what to do to save his people." Motley paused. "The world's most dangerous tyrants," he explained, "are invariably real men of vision."

"So you mean this guy was going to save those people who were sick?" asked Martin.

"No, not those people. *His* people. People like you, who weren't even born. To save *his* people, he killed off almost every person in the country. Nine hundred and ninety-six out of every thousand. I hope I'm making this clear."

Martin shook his head, and Motley sighed. "I know. It's not so clear to me either. But what happened was this: the President had the domed suburbs built to house and protect those four people out of each thousand. *His* people were going to have a great way of life. They would be the envy of the whole world."

"And they had game shows," Martin guessed, "to choose his people."

Motley nodded. "Yes, it was a big media circus."

"And everyone else, the people who lost, the people who didn't count. What did he do about them?"

"They died," Motley said. "Quickly. Many of them died right on the shows, just like they do today. Those who didn't usually paid for the privilege of dying. You see, in order to talk people into the steel suburbs and the game shows, the President convinced them that all life on Earth was going to be wiped out. The television was full of it in those days, how nobody would survive the disasters and diseases that were about to strike humankind. People were so scared that they paid to be killed painlessly; they got the shot, just like people do today. My predecessors helped quite a bit—certain members of the scientific community, that is—predicting things and then faking things like deaths by disease. The President had promised scientists their own special compounds and laboratories. And besides, they wanted to save humanity too."

"That's sick!" Martin said. "And it's crazy!"

"I'm afraid," said Motley apologetically, "that it all made quite a bit of sense."

"And then what happened?"

"Nothing," said Motley. "It's been the same ever since. The television shows have changed, and the lies have gotten older, but that's the way things are to this day. You're descended from the lucky ones, and you used to be one too. Now you're a condemned criminal, running from the law under sentence of execution."

"What?" Martin sat up straight. "Hey, wait a minute! I didn't do anything."

"Yes, you did," Motley said. "You followed me, another condemned criminal. And now you know the truth about the myths and the lies. You can't seriously imagine that a government like ours would let you live after that."

Martin already knew that, he realized. He'd known it since the blond bot had come to take him away in her special car.

Maybe he had known it since the Wonder Babies had been recalled, and he had realized that his own President could classify children as unsafe products.

"I wish you hadn't come to our suburb," he said bitterly. "You should have left us alone."

"I'm not so sure that would have saved you," Motley said. "You seem to have learned quite a bit about the lies without my help. And what about your sister, Cassie? Didn't somebody need to save her?"

"It's none of your business," Martin muttered. "She's *my* sister."

"She's mine too," Motley said. "As near as any of us comes to having a sister."

Martin glared at him. "Just how do you figure that?"

"My real name is Rudy—Rudolph Church," Motley said. "I was named for my designer. I'm a prototype, the prototype for the Wonder Babies, but when I was little, I didn't know that. I grew up in the GenLab, so I thought I was a scientist. They gave me my first lab coat when I was three.

"The Human Genetics Laboratory was an amazing place in those days, part of the larger scientific compound, which practically made up a world of its own. We scientists had done very well for ourselves under this government, and it shows in our remarkable achievements. My designer, Dr. Church, ran the GenLab for almost thirty years, and he gathered the brightest scientific minds there. They were determined to use their freedom to do what had never before been done: apply science to improve our species. And they died convinced that they had done it too, convinced that we were a generation beyond them. But when I think of their genius, I wonder. Do we surpass them?"

He looked earnestly at Martin. "I do hope that we at least equal the clarity and rapidity of their reasoning, but I fervently hope that we never equal their cruelty."

"Cruelty?" Martin said. "Their babies were a good thing. My suburb was always happy when the stork came."

"Of course you were," Rudy said. "You saw only success. But I lived in the lab, and I saw all the rest of it. The incubators that got turned off. The experiments that failed. Disease resistance, for example: How can you be sure that your designer children are genetically immune to a deadly disease? You expose them to it. If they catch it, you've learned something. The children die, and you move on. The next ones may survive."

Martin grimaced. "They *did* that?"

Rudy nodded. "I remember Dr. Church trying to explain it to me when I was small. I was missing Terence, my playmate. Terence was a prototype too, and she sang like an angel, but she couldn't learn how to read. When she disappeared, I kept looking for her, so finally Dr. Church told me. Terence was an experiment, he said, holding me on his lap, and she had been terminated that morning. All the scientists loved her very much, but they loved our species more. They had to do what was best for humanity."

"I bet!" Martin said. "Like that President and *his* people. Anybody they didn't like just didn't count. The way I see it, they're the criminals, not me. This whole place is run wrong."

"Just what someone I know used to say quite often," Rudy remarked, "but she used more colorful language. The Dish Fourteen in our lab didn't take their word on any of this. She was the oldest prototype, our big sister, and she didn't care about humanity, she cared about us. Whenever something was up, she'd find it out somehow, and then she'd come to me. 'Rudy, they met about Isadora today. You have to help me hide her.' There's nothing more loyal than a Dish Fourteen, except maybe a modified bot. I'm not surprised that an angry Fourteen has hunted me down."

"And did you?" Martin asked.

"Did I what?"

"Did you hide Isadora?"

He sighed. "Yes, we did, but sooner or later, they always found us. And I suppose that was the ultimate irony. Here this team of scientists had caused untold suffering to produce what they thought was an improvement in the species. Then they had to face the tragic fact: no one wanted their improvement!

"Oh, it sounded good to the marketers for a while. 'New and improved' always sounds good to marketers. But, ultimately, the Wonder Babies were a disaster. And by the time the scientists of the Human Genetics Lab were finished with their tinkering and inventing, they had given our government every tool it needed to treat babies as merchandise. We humans could be designed, patented, ordered, and sold under distinct product lines. And that meant we could also be recalled. So last winter, when they learned that little children were starting to ask dangerous questions, the government decided to recall the Wonder Babies."

"Last winter?" Martin interrupted. "I don't get that; I mean, about the winter part. They just had the Wonder Baby vote last week."

Rudy looked surprised. "You believe the votes get counted?"

Martin thought about that and shook his head.

"Along with the recall, we prototypes were scheduled for demolition. But the scientists refused to give us up. We were their life-work! They managed to sneak us out of the compound instead. So the government put those geniuses on the game shows, where most of them didn't last ten minutes. But Dr. Church wound up on a question-and-answer show and held off death for almost a month. I know he had done horrible things, but he was a father to me, and I loved him. I would have taken his place if I could."

"I don't see why!" Martin burst out. "How can you love a father who chooses between you and your sister? I mean, how can you even try to love someone like that?"

"By not growing up to be like him," said Rudy quietly. "At least, that's what I hope I've done. But dying for him wasn't an option. I had to rescue the Wonder Babies before the government could dispose of them. It was a tricky business. You were an anxious moment, in fact, with your talk of game shows and lab coats, but I managed to save Cassie—your sister and mine."

Martin sat frowning at the table, trying to take it all in. After a minute, Rudy got up from his chair.

"She's sure to be finished with her exam now," he said. "I'll have her called out of class."

Cassie came along a few minutes later, accompanied by another child carrying two lunches on trays. As soon as she saw Martin, she jumped up and down and squealed.

"You came, you came!" she shrieked. "My brother came to see me! I have a visitor! I'm the first student in the whole school to have a visitor!" Then she hurled herself into his arms.

Martin hugged her skinny little body and tugged a few golden curls, unable to speak at first. But William had already heard about his tears over Chip's demise. It would never do to get a reputation for being weepy.

"Well, duh, I came," he said gruffly. "I had to check this school thing out. I wasn't just going to leave it up to that rat catcher guy."

They ate ham sandwiches and fruit cups in the little room while Cassie told him about her new life. Martin let her rattle on about quadratic equations and logical paradigms without interrupting to ask for explanations. She looked happy and healthy, with pink cheeks and the start of a tan, so she wasn't spending all her time studying.

"You're wearing our uniform," she laughed, plucking at his T-shirt. "Rudy says these are the best clothes for everybody: comfortable, easy to launder, and very durable. But sometimes he still wears his lab coat. He points it out to us as a case of irrational attachment."

"I hate lab coats," Martin said with a shudder.

"I wish Mom and Dad had come too. How are they?"

"They're doing just great," Martin lied as cheerfully as he could. Then he remembered that he wasn't a very good liar. "Mom said, 'Be sure and find your sister for me and make sure she's okay.' She's really glad you're at a special school, and she hopes"—Martin choked up for a second—"she hopes you're doing math."

"Mom actually said that?" Cassie's face shone with happiness. "She always hated my math!"

"Nah," Martin said. "She was just being that way for you. She thought it was what you needed to hear. If parents told us what they really think about stuff, we could figure them out like regular people."

Then he told her about his journey and all the amazing things he had seen. He even told her about the aromatic shoe dump. But he left out the terrifying storm in the ruined suburb, and he didn't tell her that Hertz had been looking for her school. Those things were too scary for a six-year-old to hear, even if she was a genius.

Nevertheless, it was possible that Cassie guessed something about it. Certainly, she became very serious. "So much of what we learned in the suburb was wrong," she said. "It was all just fluffy lies. Like *Peter Pan*. Do you know, I've read the real *Peter Pan* now. He wasn't a lawyer at all; he was just a boy like you. And the Lost Boys weren't accountants; they were a bunch of boys who got lost. They lived together in a cave underneath a forest, and they fought Captain Hook face-to-face, with guns and swords."

"Wow!" Martin said. "That's a module I might actually like."

"You could read it if you're going to stay for a few days," Cassie said. "What are you going to do now?"

That was a good question. He had no home, no way to go back. It had all been fine as long as he had somewhere to go, but now that he had found Cassie, he had no goal.

"I dunno," he said. "I haven't really thought about it. Maybe I'll just stay here and go to school."

"You?" Cassie giggled. "Martin, you'd hate it! You couldn't even do our work."

"Well, hey, I don't just have to sit in class with you little Wonder Babies," he said, nettled. "There are older kids here too. There's William. I'm probably in her grade." For an agreeable moment, he imagined sitting behind William in class. Now, that would be a reason to go to school!

"William is a prototype more advanced than us Exponents. She doesn't go to class, she teaches. All the teachers study every day, but they don't take lessons. They team-teach one another, the way we used to do in the suburb."

"Oh, isn't that fabulous!" Martin muttered. "Just what the world needs: another brain!"

"You could still stay here," Cassie said. "I know Rudy wouldn't mind. There's lots of work to do. You could help out."

Martin imagined William standing before her class, pointing to something on a diagram: *Now, you see here that the crystalline structure comes from Na and Cl— Oh, just a minute, class. Martin's here to take out the trash.*

"As janitor to the stars, huh? Not this guy! Let those brains empty their own garbage."

"But what'll you do if you don't stay here? Maybe they're sending bots after you. It isn't safe to leave."

"That's just too bad for me, isn't it?" he snapped. "I didn't get a lucky break like having my own special school. It's a shame your brother's such a mental cripple. How embarrassing for you!"

Cassie burst into tears.

Martin hadn't risked his life and walked all that way just to make his little sister cry. He hugged her tightly.

"Hey, stop it," he begged. "I'm just being stupid. Did you know I brought your bunny all the way from home? That Rudy-Motley guy's got it."

She sobbed into the front of his shirt. "Really?" her muffled voice said. "I couldn't sleep, I missed Bun so much. And I missed you, too."

Martin swallowed the lump in his throat. "Yeah, I know. That's why I came."

Cassie dug a tissue out of her pocket and wiped her face. "It's just that I'm worried for you," she quavered. "I don't know what you're going to do." Neither did he, he reflected unhappily, but whatever happened, he was her big brother. She needed to remember him that way.

"Don't worry about me, Cass," he said. "I know how to get along out in the wilderness now. I don't need suburbs and schools. You know what? I'm just like that kid in the story, that Peter Pan."

"Can you really live like Peter Pan?" she said in wonder. "All on your own, without a pillow?"

"Sure," he said. "What do you think I did to get here, push my bed along the packet rails? While you're sitting in your classroom, learning about microbes and stuff, you think about your big brother out there living in a tree and fighting off bots with my bare hands. Maybe I'll even have my own Lost Boys."

A little smile broke through her tears, warming him with its glow. "Wow! My own brother. That's amazing!"

"Yeah," said Martin casually. "It probably seems pretty exciting to you. Hey, look, I better get going. I talked to Rudy about this place, and he seems okay. I guess I'll let him look after you. But I'll be back to make sure he doesn't get all corrupt and turn you into factory workers or something."

"Are you sure you have to leave now?" Cassie's blue eyes threatened to fill with tears again. "You haven't even met any of my new friends."

"I'm sure," Martin answered. His bravado was already trickling away, and he didn't want her to see it run out. "Gotta go while it's still daylight. I've got . . . shelters to build and stuff. And I'll bet you've got schoolwork to finish."

That helped, because of course she did. She perked up at once. Martin walked her down the hall while she described all the assignments she had to complete. So focused was he on maintaining his composure that he didn't retain a word. He couldn't even remember how her last smile looked after she hugged him good-bye.

Sim was at his elbow. "Rudy wants to see you," he said, so Martin followed him to another of the offices. Rudy sat behind a desk almost as messy as William's, and the thought of that brilliant young girl completed Martin's misery.

"I listened to your conversation with your sister," Rudy explained with a touch of remorse. "She's right; I would be glad to offer you a place here. But I heard your decision, and I understand."

Great, Martin thought. No chance now to beg for a home. It was back to the loneliness of the wide world, with only Chip for company. And Chip, unfortunately, couldn't speak.

"I just want you to know," Rudy went on, "how proud you would have made your designer. Dr. Dreyfus maintained to the end of his days that exam scores are a deceptive measure of our worth. He built into his Fourteens his own ingenuity and stubbornness, and I know humanity is richer for it."

Martin remembered the feeling of Cassie's last hug, and a lump rose in his throat. "But what good did it do?" he asked in despair. "All those guys are gone, all the baby doctors. So we're it now, the very last ones. The stork isn't ever going to come anymore." He gulped. "No more scientists. No more babies!"

Rudy watched Martin struggle against tears, and a quizzical smile played across his face. "I can appreciate your concern," he said at last. "But here's some hopeful news. If you live outside the suburbs—with their media-perfected existence, and their sedative-laced foods, and their government-mandated, automatically dosed sterilizing drugs—if you choose to abandon these little slices of heaven for a life closer to what we humans were truly meant for, then, Martin, you will find that you do not need a scientist to help you make a baby."

Martin wiped his nose. "What?" he asked.

"A logical question," Rudy admitted hastily, "but I'm afraid that's as far as it goes. Better get you off to your next adventure now; Sim will take you to your gear." And a bewildered Martin found himself once again tagging along with the elderly bot.

They came to a very large room that apparently served as the cafeteria. At this time of day, all the benches were empty, and only one other person was in sight. She had poured the contents of Hertz's knapsack onto one of the tables and laid the gear out in neat piles. Just now, she was hefting the skillet with the folding handle. Martin was incensed.

"Hey, that's my stuff!" he shouted, charging across the lunchroom.

"And heaven forbid I should touch your stuff," she replied with perfect composure. She put the pan down and picked up a small container. "Do you have any idea what this does? No? Well, neither do I."

After the incredibly beautiful people he had seen that day, this woman was refreshingly plain, but for all that, she still didn't look ordinary. She had olive skin, a stubby nose, and a mouth that looked as if, whether it smiled or frowned, it would do so only on its own terms. Her black hair was clipped like a man's and graying at the temples, even though she couldn't have been older than thirty. She was short, and her bones were strong and compact. They gave her an active, vigorous appearance, like a rubber ball that would bounce right back if it got thumped.

She put down the mysterious container and looked at him. Her eyes were dark hazel, just like his, light brown with green and gold flecks.

"I heard what you said to your sister."

"Did anybody *not* hear what I said to Cassie?" Martin groaned. "I should have been on television!"

"I'd have sat through it twice," said the woman. "What's eating you? Oh, I get it. You've just been talking to Rudy. Young Church Junior is a sweetheart, but he can be a major downer. That's a Wonder Baby for you. Those guys get emotional over prime numbers."

"Yeah," agreed Martin, cheered by the analysis. "Yeah, that's my sister, too." He watched the woman make a thoughtful face, pursing her lips, as she held a medicine bottle up to the light.

"We Fourteens don't think like that," she observed as she put it down. "We don't sit around and feel life's pain. We just live. We get on with it."

"Hey, are you a Fourteen too?"

Her face lit up with a shrewd grin, and the flecks in her hazel eyes gleamed like sparks. "You're *a* Fourteen," she said, snapping her finger against his shoulder. "I'm *the* Fourteen. I'm the prototype for all you little babies. My name's Theo—Theodore Dreyfus. I was named for my designer."

"Theo?" Martin felt the grin spread across his face.

The woman gave him an appraising glance. "You've got any funny things to say about my name, you get them out of your system right now," she advised. "You didn't say anything smart to William, I noticed. You just stared at her like she was solid gold." She tumbled a set of nesting cups out of their case and squinted at one of the labels.

Martin felt his face heat up until the insides of his ears were on fire. "Crap!" he said bitterly. "Does everybody just mind *everybody's* business around here?"

"Don't talk to me about privacy," said Theo with passion. "You didn't grow up in a lab. You don't even know what privacy means, young man, until you catch a team of scientists sneaking into your locker after lights-out, trying to steal the key to your diary. But enough of this chitchat. Down to brass tacks. Did you chicken out or are you really taking off?"

Feeling forlorn again, Martin sat down on the nearest bench. "I'm really taking off," he answered.

"I knew it!" She smiled to herself. "Well, as it happens, so am I."

"You are?" Martin stared at her. "Why?"

"Two reasons. We protos held a meeting, and we're worried about the school. You found it fast enough—of course, you *are* a Fourteen—but still, we need a safer place. I'm heading out in the morning to look for one.

"And the second reason . . ." She stopped looking through the camping equipment and dropped down onto the bench beside him. "We Fourteens," she explained in a low voice, "just hate school as it is. And this place is like your ultimate school. When I see all these little copies of Rudy running around, clutching their handhelds and holding the doors open for me, it's like I'm stuck inside a bad horror movie. I can only take it for a couple of days, and then I have got to get out."

Martin laughed. "I know just how you feel!"

"Well, if you can handle this place for one more night, you can come with me in the morning. Just think about it." She resumed her work.

Martin watched her repack the camping gear, feeling pleased about life. He had an exciting mission ahead of him, and the way news traveled around here, odds were good that William had already heard about it.

Sim opened the door of the cafeteria, and a large shape hurtled through. It made straight for Martin, howling madly, and swept him off the bench. He struggled to get up, fending off the attack with both arms, but he didn't have much success.

"Your bot is recharged," Sim said helpfully, bending over him. "But I gather you know that already."

"That thing is a *dog*?" Theo said. "You've got to be kidding me! It's got two circuit boards and enough fancy chips to be the President and three of his special prosecutors."

Martin struggled to his knees and threw his arms around the ecstatic German shepherd. "Don't you listen to her, Chip," he said. "You don't want to be the President. Anybody can do that, even bad guys can do it, but who else can be the world's best dog? Stop fooling around now. Act serious for a second and promise me you're never gonna change."

Chip's wagging tail was the only answer he needed.

ABOUT THE AUTHOR

CLARE B. DUNKLE STUDIED RUSSIAN AND LATIN AT TRINITY UNIVERSITY IN TEXAS, AND ALSO HOLDS A MASTER'S DEGREE IN LIBRARY SCIENCE FROM INDIANA UNIVERSITY. SHE NOW LIVES WITH HER FAMILY IN OBERMOHR, GERMANY.

UNWIND
By Neal Shusterman

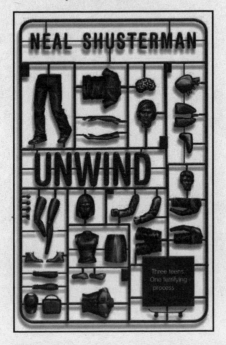

In a society where unwanted teens are salvaged
for their body parts, three teen runaways fight
the system that would unwind them.

If they can survive until their eighteenth birthdays,
they can't be harmed. But when every piece of them,
from their hands to their hearts, is the legal property
of the government, that day seems a long way off...

A breath-taking, futuristic thriller, challenging accepted
notions about life and death, and questioning what it
truly means to be alive.

ISBN: 978-1-84738-231-3
Price: £6.99